TWO FOR THE TABLELANDS

Kevin Major

The author thanks members of the RCMP and the RNC who generously answered his research questions (and who, he is quick to note, bear no resemblance to the police officers in the book). Thanks go out as well to the fine team at Breakwater, and especially to editor Marnie Parsons for her keen eye and attention to detail. It's all left Sebastian anxious for the author to get on with the next case.

BREAKWATER
P.O. Box 2188, St. John's, NL, Canada, A1C 6E6
WWW.BREAKWATERBOOKS.COM

A CIP CATALOGUE RECORD FOR THIS BOOK IS AVAILABLE FROM LIBRARY AND ARCHIVES CANADA

COPYRIGHT © 2020 Kevin Major
ISBN 978-1-55081-844-4

Cover photograph by Colin Peddle

ALL RIGHTS RESERVED. No part of this publication may be reproduced, stored in a retrieval system or transmitted, in any form or by any means, without the prior written consent of the publisher or a licence from The Canadian Copyright Licensing Agency (Access Copyright). For an Access Copyright licence, visit www.accesscopyright.ca or call toll free to 1-800-893-5777.

We acknowledge the support of the Canada Council for the Arts. We acknowledge the financial support of the Government of Canada and the Government of Newfoundland and Labrador through the Department of Tourism, Culture, Industry and Innovation for our publishing activities.
PRINTED AND BOUND IN CANADA.

Breakwater Books is committed to choosing papers and materials for our books that help to protect our environment. To this end, this book is printed on a recycled paper that is certified by the Forest Stewardship Council®.

Second Printing

attaboy, Gaffer, writing pal

It was the difference between ochre and umber. Between yellow iron oxide and red iron oxide. Between his skin and the thick stain of his blood.

It was Nick who stumbled upon the body. Not something the young fellow needed to see—a naked man half buried by rocks nearly the colour of his skin, skin tarnished by a discharge of blood sun-dried to a semblance of clay.

The body was meant to go unnoticed and might have done so for days had Nick not gone off poking around after our swim.

He yelled for me, panicked. I plowed back into my hiking boots and raced over the rocks thinking he was in danger, had fallen, had fractured a bone.

Goddamn.

I turned Nick's head away. There were enough gaps in the rocks heaped on the body that it was obvious the fellow's throat had been slit, the bloodied flesh contracted from exposure, but gaping wide. A corpse partially covered by rocks, a game plan that ran out of time. An abandoned burial mound. One arm in view but not the other, a section of thigh, a twisted angle of leg, a foot. A half-exposed, crushed penis.

Goddamn.

1

I AM INCREASINGLY freaked by heights.

Which has a lot to do with the fact that last year I skidded, scraped, and plummeted down a near-perpendicular drop of thirty metres, and lived. I was never predisposed to heights, but now they do very weird things to my head. And my intestines. I steer clear of ledges.

Of which there is no shortage in Newfoundland.

Nicholas, my freshly teenaged son, seems not to have inherited that gene. Following in the footsteps of his mother, so to speak. Samantha, when she was also my wife, was forever one to lead me to precipitous circumstances.

I digress.

Which brings me to the reason I now find myself, this Thanksgiving weekend, climbing Gros Morne, the second highest peak in Newfoundland. To be precise it is not really a *peak*. More of a pink, bald-headed *noggin* that rises within the confines of Gros Morne National Park, spectacular though it is in its own way.

Nicholas is impressed. Thirteen-year-olds, I know full well, are not easily impressed. It's their hormonal predisposition to be underwhelmed. Having once been a teacher, I know of what I speak. Grade Eight (from which Nick recently emerged, generally unscathed as far as I can tell, though the jury is still out) is universally thought of among teachers as "the lost year." Puberty has kicked in and unsuspecting trainees turn hopelessly oddball. A few months into Grade Nine and said adolescents are usually set to rejoin the human race.

'This is fun,' says Nicholas, as we ascend a kilometre of scree consisting of hefty fragments of blasted quartzite left by receding glaciers. "Fun" is such an all-encompassing descriptor. I prefer "interesting," or, more precisely, "strenuously interesting."

The fifty-ish father cannot, however, let on that he might not be totally up for the task at hand. 'Sure is,' I manage, between somewhat laboured breaths. Fortunately the son, the veritable billy goat, is several steps ahead and not party to my panting.

We have already hiked four kilometres through forest and flies to get to the base of the peak. The rock-strewn ascent does have enough wind to keep the flies at bay, which is no mean boost to my overall well-being. Life will be grand, I am supremely confident, once we get to the top.

It's pushing an hour and a half. Just when you think you will go no higher, a new expanse of damned blasted quartzite reveals itself. On top of that, the wind goes from fly-inhibiting to stiff and chilled. The temperature has dropped, rain threatens, and devilishly thick accumulations of low clouds (i.e., fog) look about to join us for the last few metres to the top.

We are finally at the proof of our climb, the substantial sign that reads Gros Morne Summit 806 m/*Sommet Gros-Morne 806 m*. The fact that it is the same elevation in both English and French is nothing if not a stimulant for the tired mind.

'A little closer, if you would,' I say to the overly fit senior who has offered to take a picture of the mountain-conquering duo with my iPhone. At that distance the sign should be readable through fog.

Followed by the inevitable smiling selfie. Followed by, 'Okay, now let's eat.'

It's amazing what a teenage male can pack away on a couch watching TV, let alone after climbing 806 m. Up to this point I have fended off all calls for sustenance except for water and trail mix. But as Nick likes to elucidate, 'This dude is in the mood for food.'

Fortunately our combined backpacks approach the size of a small refrigerator, and Nick can feast on a range of consumables—sausages, sandwiches, hard-boiled eggs, fruit, cheese sticks, crackers and hummus, beef jerky, celery wisely filled with peanut butter, muffins, cookies, Gatorade.

Life is indeed grand, and even more so when something amazing, if not altogether surprising, happens. (We're talking Newfoundland weather after all, as changeable as a dog's stomach.) The fog lifts, the sun struggles to show itself, and, in the end, does. A stunning vista unfolds. One of the iconic views of Gros Morne National Park.

I'm fired up to be sharing it with my son. We sit and absorb the amazing panorama of Ten Mile Pond. A long stretch of sun-glinting, fjord-like blue water at a mountain base of forest green, ascending to bald cliffs.

'We're talking the Long Range Mountains, the northeastern end of the Appalachians. Those cliffs you see before you—granitic gneiss.'

'Nice.'

'Yep, the 'g' is silent—gneiss.'

'No, I mean, nice. Nice, man, way to go. You read the guidebook. Nice.'

At least two minutes pass before he gives into the paralyzing urge to find out if there is cell phone reception.

'Tyler, man, guess where I am?' Pause. 'Keep it clean.'

I can only imagine.

'No, man, on top of Gros Morne.' Pause. Laughter. 'The mountain, man.'

What else?

'Yes, really. With my dad. I know. Nice.'

Nice is good.

'You wish. Okay, gotta go.' Pause. 'I will.'

It's all downhill from here, literally. In fact the descent down the back of the mountain and around the base to the starting point is positively endless. It runs us four hours at least. But when we do finally reach the parking lot, the food supply completely depleted (including, finally, the celery sticks), Nick is still in a decent mood. Hungry, but not whining. Which I take as a sign that he is no longer a kid. Manhood in the offing.

'Yes, we did it!' High fives.

'Whomped it good!' High fives again. 'This dude....'

I know. 'Is in the mood...'

'For food.'

Which means I have to make good on my promise, made halfway down the mountain, to forego our own kitchen skills in favour of the Old Loft Restaurant in Woody Point.

It's a costly trait that I've encouraged in Nick—to get past fried chicken, tacos, and pizza, to take some risks in what he puts in his gut. When he stays over at my house we make a regular habit of cooking together, kitchen buds working up a recipe from a cookbook, or snagging one off the Internet. Culinary bonding.

Last Christmas I gave him a cookbook. Really. Well, there was more stuff, but I thought give my kid a cookbook and I'm making a statement. So he shows up the following week with the book in his sports bag and a square of toilet paper as a bookmark for the recipe he'd like to try.

I'm fired up, and instead of me going out New Year's Eve to some party where at midnight I kiss women who play on my imagination, Nick and I cook up something called "Double Whammy Toad in the Hole." (Jamie Oliver—I like his cookbooks, not too keen on his kitchen knives.) My take is that Nick chose it because it sounds and looks slightly vulgar, and among the ingredients is a can of beer.

But, hey, he's fired up too, and actually "Double Whammy Toad in the Hole" is pretty decent. We scoffed the lot while watching the mega, multi-coloured crystal ball drop in Times Square.

Ravenous Gaffer gets off on it as well. The dog always was a sucker for sausages. He also enjoys free-range eggs, and has been known to have the odd lick of beer. Given that he's renounced kibble since the day Nick and I brought him home from the SPCA, you could say he was in doggie heaven. It will no doubt go down as one of his most memorable New Year's Eves.

In the Old Loft Restaurant, the mountaineers dig into traditional Newfoundland fare. That would be moose pie and salad for me, and for the young fellow fish cakes, baked beans, and bread baked right on the premises. And a cut each of partridgeberry pie and ice cream. We're keeners for a good scoff.

'Gaffer would love this,' says Nick, in a brief, doleful respite between mouthfuls.

He misses the mutt, as do I. But Gaffer's doing fine. He's staying with my friend Jeremy while we're away.

Nick takes a picture of his plate of food and fires it off to Jeremy, with a note to Gaffer. 'Wish I could send you a doggie bag.'

He sends the same picture off to his friend Tyler. His phone dings in about ten seconds. 'Tyler says gross.' He adds, 'Tyler can't see past burgers and fries. Sad, very sad.'

That's my boy. And for that, young Nick, on our way out of the restaurant we get a loaf of the homemade bread and a jar of bakeapple jam for breakfast in the morning.

We hit the road and find our way to the cabin we have rented for three days. So far it's been a father-son expedition to remember.

On the agenda for the following day is a hike to Green Gardens, another jewel of the National Park. Green Gardens has two possible routes. For a fall day it's a hot one (relatively speaking, which in Newfoundland means anything approaching 20°C), so we opt for the shorter hike, nine kilometres return. I'm still in recovery mode from the trek up Gros Morne. I didn't sleep well last night. Recurring dreams in which I kept climbing and climbing and never reaching the top.

As the brochure promises, today's hike takes us across "a barren landscape of frost-cracked orange-brown peridotite boulders."

'Easy for you to say.' He chuckles. 'Good one, Nicholas.'

Complimenting himself, as teenagers are prone to do. Possibly to stroke his ego, more likely, as we say, for a laugh. Chip off the old block.

We're having fun. And yes, an hour later and we're still having fun. Much of the hike is downhill, through boreal forest, which can be a bit scruffy, mostly coniferous—black spruce, balsam fir, and juniper (what mainlanders have christened larch or tamarack). None of it very tall, and a lot of it windblown. With a few birch and alder mixed in, lots of ferns and moss. A promising habitat for wildlife. We're hoping moose or caribou, but would settle for a fox or a mink. Squirrels and shrews don't count.

And a red fox it is, and a fine fellow at that. He lingers in view for longer than I expect. Nick is scrambling for his phone to take a picture, but I silently wave him off. He shrugs. We stand motionless together and watch the fox stare back at us for a few seconds before disappearing into the undergrowth.

'I coulda got a great picture.'

'But this was better. Just man and fox. Eye to eye.'

'Whatever.'

'Life is not meant to be experienced behind a camera lens. You're putting up a barrier. Hold on to the moment for what it is.' My little life lesson for the day.

'Really?' He's not convinced. But then, he's at the age when he is not convinced by much. But neither does he argue. This is good.

We break out of the boreal forest to a cliff-top sweep of fertile green meadow. There's the odd sheep grazing, likely brought in for the summer from a community nearby. The one closest to us looks up and, unimpressed by the appearance of yet another hiker, tucks his head back in the grass and chews on.

'He's not very photogenic anyway,' says Nick, straining to hold back his grin.

Smartass. I wring a fist playfully at him.

Nick throws off his backpack. Jumps into a martial arts position, as if he had training when all he's ever done is watch a few movies.

'C'mon, sucker, let's see what you're made of!' Followed by a few combative grunts.

'Really?' A slow, very broad smile. My backpack falls from my shoulders. My hands calmly rise, the fingers flexing in the call to combat.

'Let's see what's behind that gut of yours!'

'Dangerous, Nicky boy, very dangerous.'

In one swift move he's flattened in the grass. He is ticklish as hell and I make him pay dearly for the gut comment.

'Say uncle.'

'What?'

'Say uncle.'

'What's that supposed to mean?'

He's never heard it before? 'It means you give up.'

'Back in the day, it did. That dates you, old man.'

Another dig in the ribs. He's still laughing when I let him up, and back to martial arting.

'So what's your equivalent of "say uncle"?'

'You don't want to know.'

He's right. I probably don't.

There's stairs to the beach. And just out from the beach, a cluster of sea stacks—tall, lumpy, vaguely monstrous. Unlike anything he's ever seen.

'And you saw plenty of sea stacks…back in the day,' says Nick.

'Okay, dickhead…'

'You're calling your own son a dickhead? What kind of father are you?'

'One who's about to dive into the water, not like you, dickhead.'

I throw down the backpack and start unlacing my hiking boots.

'That water is cold as hell. You're crazy.'

'And you're chicken.'

And the race is on. In the end we're both flailing about in the Atlantic Ocean, which is bloody well frigid. 'Cold enough to freeze the balls off a brass monkey. As we used to say.'

'Back in the day.'

Nicholas is a good kid. Cheeky at times, but that's par for the course. I want him growing up with the reassurance that his father will always be there for him, despite everything that has gone on between his mother and me. The marriage crashed, and any effort to hold it together for Nick's sake would never have yielded anything but warfare. Who wants to put a kid through that? We have shared custody. It's not perfect, but you make do.

Life goes on. We all survive. And in this instance, I freeze my ass off so he gets the point that I would go to the end of the earth to make sure he grows up a happy, well-adjusted kid.

Which is where we find ourselves on our last day in Gros Morne. Hiking the Tablelands is not going to the end of the earth, but having the end of the earth come to us.

It's one of the few places on planet earth where the mantle has erupted through its crust and come to rest on the surface. One for the books. A bona fide, 500-million-year-old geological stunner. What we have today is a vast, almost plant-less, flat-top, yellow-oxided mountainscape. Looking for all the world like a desert, but, even after summer, still with patches of snow filling its uppermost basins.

'Weird, eh?'

I expect more of my son. He lives in Newfoundland and he doesn't get excited by rock? What a waste of a birthplace.

'You might call it quote/unquote *weird*. Geologists call it phenomenal.'

'Listen, Tyler, we're in this *phenomenal* place called the Tablelands.'

The damn phone again. Deep breath. Control yourself, Sebastian.

'Snow. Yes, snow. I can see it. Yes, we're climbing up there.'

Am I in for a running commentary as we ascend the mountain? I don't get it. Why is his life permanently on "share"?

'Nick, pal, put away the phone. Give it a rest.'

He consents, a little grudgingly, but does finally slip it into a pocket. He doesn't say anything. That, too, is good.

So the primordial technology of the ultra-lightweight, simple-to-store Parks Canada pamphlet tells us the best route to the top of the Tablelands is to start to the left of Wallace Brook where it crosses the footpath leading from the parking lot.

The route is unsigned, undefiled, and relatively untrodden.

At least there are no others setting out the same time we do. The hike is largely over peridotite, its surface this time oxidized to a sweep of yellowish tan. A vast geological coup, a sublime triumph of beige.

The mantle rock erupted to the surface when ancient continents collided. Living proof of continental drift. Well, not living, since the only thing living is at the base of the Tablelands, a scattered few low-growing shrubs and plants that somehow survived the near toxic scrapings of soil and sub-arctic winter wind and weather.

'Tough little buggers,' I call them. Nick agrees. I am tempted to capture some of the diminutive alpine species that contrast with the rock, but my phone must remain firmly out of sight.

Nick knows what is going through my mind, knows I get off on plants when I have the time. He grins a self-satisfied grin.

Ignored. 'Holding on to the moment,' I tell him, and return the grin, substantially wider than his own. Bugger.

It's about a kilometre to what is referred to as the Lower Bowl, a steady trek over chunky peridotite. Nick is playing the young goat once again, although this time, the incline being more age-friendly, I'm almost a match for him. Almost.

He's near the rim of the Bowl, waiting for me along the edge of the brook we have been following much of the way. He's settled in for some grub. No sign of the phone, not to say there hasn't been a clandestine text before I got there.

It's sweatshirt weather, the temperature modulated by the increasing altitude and the snow patches. Still, the brook, in the few places where the water has pooled, looks enticing. Maybe on the way down.

For now, something to relieve the shameless appetite. It's been two hours since breakfast after all. Cashews and the ever manly, protein-packed beef jerky.

Nick grabs the package and begins reading the back of it.

TWO FOR THE TABLELANDS

I've taught him well. 'You know this stuff is packed with salt, fat, and sodium nitrate. Sounds like a recipe for a heart attack.'

Taught him too well. I have no defense. 'Sometimes you gotta take one for the team.'

We strike strips of jerky as if they were wine glasses. 'Chin! Chin!' I vow to eat some raw broccoli as penance.

The snow in the Bowl is not far off, so we start making tracks. We jump rocks to cross the stream and Nick races for the chance at a snowball fight. The little sucker's got a better arm than I gave him credit for. It's more like ice crystals and still damn cold, even though the air temp is mostly comfortable.

As enticing as it is to traverse the snow patch, it's not such a bright idea. Snow melting beneath could cause a section of it to collapse. Don't want to end up in an icebox. Instead, we skirt its edge and continue the climb, passing a few people on their way down, and pressing on to where there's no going any higher.

The view over Bonne Bay is brilliant. It's one of the most beautiful small bays in Newfoundland. Several communities trail its shoreline and in the distance beyond them is Gros Morne, the mountain, challenged and conquered two days ago.

It does a father and his son good to sit among the peridotite and take in the mighty geological forces at play on this earth of ours. Here we are perched atop a profound seismic event, now a UNESCO World Heritage Site, yet, in the grand scheme— we're mere specks in time and place. And to think that we're drifting apart from Eurasia still, at the rate of two and a half centimetres a year!

'Anything left to eat?'

The endless gut sharpens reality. The view before us apparently a limited distraction.

The salt and preservative-ridden jerky has long disappeared. As have the granola bars. I'm afraid we're down to the dried fruit and raw veg department. Figs and carrot sticks. Which elicit an audible groan.

I offer up five minutes of phone time as compensation. Manna from heaven. Good God, it's as if I had unwrapped a Mars bar and presented it to him on a silver platter.

There's got to be an academic paper in this somewhere. A scientific comparison between cell phone usage and teenage food consumption. Maybe there's even calorie-loss potential for the obese. The iPhone denial diet. Has a certain ring to it.

The descent is less taxing than the ascent. But navigating the uneven rock and loose gravel, with legs not as quick-witted as they once were, makes for something less than a piece of cake. Better safe than a twisted ankle.

Of course young Bucky is well ahead. Likely he's been dodging over the rocks and texting at the same time. He cuts back across the stream well ahead of me, and when I reach the spot where we had stopped on the way up, he's sitting there, his sweatshirt off in anticipation that we'll make good on our plan to cool off in the shallow pool.

It means easing our way down several metres of a rocky embankment. Not particularly steep, but a bit tricky. Not that the cloven hoofed among us have any problem.

Nick has rid himself of his footwear by the time I catch up. The pool is sun-glinting and fresh, totally inviting. Neither of us anticipated a need to bring swim trunks. We look around as we scale down to our boxers. There's been no one in sight for ages.

Nick strikes a foot in the water and quickly recoils. 'Dad, man, I don't know about this.'

'There's only one way in, Nick!' Which means a deep intake of air, an ungainly scuff over the rocks, and a horizontal lunge into the deepest part.

Cold as all hell and capable of shrivelling cast iron!

He knows I'll pulverize him with water, so better to get it

over with. Nick plunges in and shoots back up, all in one motion, screeching with everything his lungs can hold. 'Ho-ly shit!'

He stays all of ten seconds. Deed done, point made, he's back onshore, rubbing himself down with his sweat shirt. Then off he hobbles, a goose-fleshed stick of a kid, Blundstones and boardshorts in hand, to find someplace halfway secluded.

I'm afraid I'm not quite so modest. There's a lot to be said for standing unabashedly naked on rocks from the earth's mantle, even if it is only for a few seconds, until I get back into hiking shorts. There's a certain cosmic karma to it. Something primal. Man transcending time and fashion.

All that suddenly pitched aside.

'DAAAD!' Laced in terror.

What the fuck! 'I'm coming!' He's injured. Sounding worse than that. I force my way into my hiking boots, knowing I'll never be able to run over the rocks without them.

I find him standing motionless, unhurt, thank God. Dressed, his hair askew, his faded t-shirt clinging to him where he hasn't completely dried himself.

'Nick, what's...'

His hand clenches my arm.

'Oh, Jesus.'

I force his head into my chest. In front of us, mostly under rock, is a body, its throat slashed. Jesus. Hideous, and for the first few seconds incomprehensible.

The poor bugger's face is covered. But not his throat. That is thrown back at an angle that widens the gash obscenely.

The edges have constricted in the sun, the flesh surrounding it caked with blood dried to earth red. Hardly any contrast to the shadowed, rusted colour of the rocks.

So little difference between the colour of the rocks and the colour of the dead man's skin that Nick had stepped on the leg before he saw the severed throat. Whoever had piled on the rocks must have run off before the job was done, leaving in view a section of the other thigh, an arm, and, crudely confirming it to be a man, an unpulverized top half of his penis.

Cringe and groan. Not something man or boy needs to see in his lifetime. Makes a fellow think twice about exposing his own boxered member on the Tablelands ever again.

Arm around his shoulder, I steer Nick away from the scene. He's shaking still.

911. A cop gets back to me, then someone from Parks Canada to establish where we are exactly. I bolster Nick back up the incline, all the time trying to talk him down from his shock.

There's a boulder big enough to seat both of us, from where we will be able to sight the cops as they make their way in our direction.

'You okay?'

He nods, unconvincingly. 'Gross,' he says. The all-encompassing word. I'm thinking he's seen worse in movies, on the Internet. Painful to witness, oddly reassuring that the real thing unsettles him.

A bit too much. He starts to cry and is shaking more than ever. I dig out the windbreaker that's in the bottom of my backpack and get him into it. Far too big of course, the sleeves ending past his hands. He settles against my chest, trying to control his sobs, wiping his snotnose in the sleeve of the jacket. Now, again, very much the kid.

'It's okay, Nick.' I hold his head to me and lean my cheek into the top of it.

I was thirty before I saw a dead person, and that was an aunt who looked better in her casket than she did in real life. What Nick saw will stick with him for a long time. But I'll hold him for all I'm worth when he needs it, and together we'll get him through this. That's what fathers are supposed to be good at.

2

RURAL NEWFOUNDLAND FALLS under the very watchful eye of the Royal Canadian Mounted Police. The Mounties. No longer much given to horses, however.

Constable Trottier (no pun intended) arrives on foot. 'From Saskatchewan,' she volunteers. 'My first week in the province.'

Not the least bit out of breath, I will add. Standard shirt under a dark blue, well-equipped vest, pants with yellow stripe the length of the leg, yellow-banded regulation field service cap. Sam Browne belt and holstered gun.

She looks lovely.

With her, and obviously in charge, is Staff Sergeant Todd MacAvery, cool and efficient, and from some place unknown. Together with two staff from Parks Canada.

Nick and I have been waiting for over an hour. What the frig took the staff sergeant so long to get it together, when someone has obviously been murdered, is beyond me. The cop station is in Rocky Harbour, on the other side of the bay, I am finally told. No doubt the sergeant instructed Parks personnel not to proceed to the potential crime scene until the police arrived to accompany them.

'Your name, please.' The staff sergeant has a notebook out, pen in hand. While a dead body waits.

'Sebastian Synard.' Always a slight embarrassment. I spell it before he asks. 'My son's name is Nicholas.'

'Your ages and place of residence.' Good God.

Nick decides to answer for himself, before I have the chance to erupt. He answers MacAvery's questions with an eagerness I would not have thought possible even ten minutes before. No, he didn't see anyone other than his father. No, he wasn't doing anything except walking around. 'Well, not really, nothing other than…' He looks at me. 'Texting…my friend Tyler.'

'And you stopped when you discovered what appeared to be a body under the rocks?'

'Of course he stopped. He was traumatized!' I try to rein myself in. 'Sergeant MacAvery, shouldn't we just proceed to the scene.'

He looks up from his notebook. 'It is important that we first establish a few facts.'

Which I take means making sure we're not two bloody loonies with a bogus story that's taking up their valuable time. All this from a cop who probably cut his friggin teeth on speeding tickets and salmon poaching.

I look over at Constable Trottier. I get the feeling she might be on my side. There's an anxiousness in her stance. Restrained, and slightly chomping at the bit. The park staff, too. It's likely there hasn't been this damn much excitement in the park since its UNESCO designation.

We do eventually make a move. Nick and I positioned between the RCMP and the Parks Canada duo, whose names by now have been revealed as Sandy and Jean-Claude. Sounds very outdoorsy, bilingual, park-like. Sandy is wearing her sandy-coloured hair in a pony tail, all the better to trek over uneven ground. Jean-Claude has sharp features, a high forehead, and indeed also has a pony tail. Though one less prone to swinging than his partner's.

We make our way down the incline, stopping at the bottom, from where I point out the pool of water in which Nick and I had our swim. Not that there is any other place it could have been.

'Cold,' says Sandy, in a slightly disapproving tone, notification that Parks Canada prefers it when visitors keep to the standard procedure of climbing up the mountain and climbing back down again. No side excursions.

'And Nick, you went off to change back into your clothes?'
'Yes, sir.'
'And what about you Mr. Synard.'
'I stayed here.'
'You changed in the open?'
'There was no one around.'

MacAvery makes a note of it.

'I'm not an exhibitionist.' Which comes out sounding defensive. 'I was in a hurry. I was cold.'

He makes another note. Pervert.

You're overreacting, Synard. Get yourself under control.

We move along, me leading the way. I bring them all to a halt. 'Nick, I want you to stay here. Everyone else, you should prepare yourselves. It's not pretty.'

MacAvery doesn't take easily to relinquishing command. As head of a crack four-person police detachment in Rocky Harbour, Newfoundland, he is used to being in control. He speeds ahead.

But comes up rather abruptly. I would say the squelched penis did the job.

The others ease their way into a viewing position on either side of him.

'Jesus,' intones MacAvery. Precisely. I would feel even more vindicated if it wasn't all so macabre.

Constable Trottier's uniformed poise is lost. Her face stiffens, the grotesqueness tossing her off her game. Sandy covers her mouth with her hand. '*Tabarnak de câlice de crisse.* Shit, shit, shit,' mutters Jean-Claude, in a deft display of his bilingualism.

Not a pretty sight. But nevertheless, any doubts that I might have been fraudulent in my claims of vile murder on the Tablelands have been emphatically dispelled.

As disgusting as it is, attention turns to the slit throat. Oddly enough, there seems to be little discharge of blood, other than the thick spill around the immediate area of the neck and chest. No trail of red over the rocks, leading to my observation that he must have been lying on the ground before his throat was sliced open.

MacAvery is not keen on me suggesting any such thing. Inappropriate, it would appear. Speculation in the case of criminal activity is the absolute purview of the police.

He doesn't realize I'm a licensed private investigator. Yes, Staff Sergeant MacAvery, there are other minds at work in the world of crime than those of the RCMP.

'Dad,' yells Nick from behind us, 'do they know you're a private eye?'

They do now.

'Really, Mr. Synard?' There can only be one person behind the question.

'Yes, really.'

'He hasn't had a case yet,' Nick throws forward, 'but he's expecting one any day now.'

My hand slips behind my back and quickly works itself into a fist. Raised a blooming little motormouth and living to regret it.

'Just recently certified. My company doesn't have a presence as yet. We are in the process of building our brand.'

'Very good.'

I think so. (*My company* meaning *me*. *We* meaning *my MacBook and I*.)

Back to the case at hand. I'm feeling the morbidity of the cut throat a little less. That comes with experience, I assume. The question is why would the killer leave the throat so obviously exposed when he/she took pains to cover most of the rest of the victim? The skin colour is more greyish now, a significant change from what it was an hour ago. Does that mean when Nick came upon him, he was not long dead? And why the direct assault on the poor fellow's hardware? Smashed rock against rock.

'Should we remove the rock covering his head?' It seems the least we could do to restore him some dignity.

MacAvery looks at me like I've asked the stupidest question possible.

'Don't anybody disturb the crime scene,' he announces. 'Constable Trottier may need assistance securing the perimeter. I have to make a few phone calls.' MacAvery walks off for some privacy. No doubt to call regional headquarters to confirm he knows his ass from a hole in the ground.

A boundary is established using a roll of yellow tape. *BARRAGE POLICIER—NE PAS TRAVERSER.* I guess they ran out of the English version. Jean-Claude is pleased and Constable Trottier doesn't really notice, preoccupied as she is with looking professional when there is nothing to tie the tape to. The only choice is to lay it along the ground, weigh it down at intervals with rock, all the while ignoring the fact that a mutilated corpse lies a few feet away. I offer to help, as do the others, positioning ourselves in the three other corners to establish a rectangle. I nod reassuringly to the constable when all is secured.

She relaxes enough that I can slip in the question that has been hounding me since she introduced herself. 'Are you by any chance related to Bryan Trottier?'

The hockey player, from the 70s and 80s, also from Saskatchewan. My boyhood hero.

'I was never quite sure.'

I look suitably confused.

'My dad always claimed we were. My mom—she said he was making it up. He desperately wanted to be. You know.'

'He still holds the NHL record for the most points in a single period.'

'Four goals and two assists.'

The ice has been soundly broken, though I can't believe we're talking hockey next to a dead body. That's Canada for you. Hockey does have that power to draw people together under the roughest of circumstances.

I should really be checking on Nick, but I can see that he's jabbering away on his phone. It's probably good for him. Takes his mind off it.

'Constable Trottier…'

'Natasha Trottier.' She extends her hand.

Very nice. I have a feeling that Natasha is not as young as she looks. And she has no ring on her finger, not that it's an absolute indicator of anything.

The staff sergeant returns, and Natasha returns to being Constable Trottier. MacAvery slips his cell phone in a pocket.

'An ambulance is on the way. The Deer Lake detachment is sending in some extra muscle to get him out.' Sandy agrees to go back to the parking lot, meet the ambulance team, and lead them to our little gathering. She's off, happy enough to be breathing untroubled air again.

'I've also asked for additional personnel to do a thorough search of the area for possible evidence. A murder weapon of course, clothing, footprints. I ask that no one go poking around on his own and compromise the crime scene.' The comment sounding suspiciously like it's directed at me. 'The crime scene will need to be thoroughly photographed. In anticipation of that I've brought along the detachment's camera. Constable Trottier will take over those duties.' He retrieves a small carrying case, which he hands to her.

I glance at Natasha. News to her, obviously. The crap jobs always fall to the new person on staff. MacAvery will want close-ups. Grisly and in sharp focus.

I let it be known that I have significant photographic experience. Going all the way back to high school when I was official photographer for the yearbook, and I have not been without a reasonably good camera since that time.

'This is police work, I'm afraid, only to be undertaken by a member of the force. Regulations, as you will appreciate.'

I do. I also appreciate, given how Natasha is holding the camera (a Nikon, which, by the way, is far more expensive and complicated than it needs to be for this job), that she hardly has a sweet clue how to operate it. On top of which, there's a very good chance that what she is about to photograph will make her nauseated. Would the good staff sergeant like the crime scene to be compromised by the constable's vomit?

If I'm pissed by MacAvery's take-charge approach, it's because underlying it is the fact that he is just as alarmed and agitated about what happened as we all are, only he's not about to admit it. A man has been murdered, his throat carved open and set on display, as is his wretched other external body part. The quicker the officer gets to the direct investigation of the murder, the better the chance the murderer hasn't hopped the ferry to Nova Scotia, skipped the province, boarded a flight in Halifax for Heathrow, connected to God-knows-where, never to be seen again.

I am not being a prejudiced jerk when I think that the victim's skin colour played a role in the murder. My theory is that whoever did it figured he struck it lucky—relatively remote location that gave him time to do the deed and let his warped instincts play out, then left in the end with a mutilated, naked body that just happened to blend in with the rockscape.

There was no way to get the body off the mountain without being seen. There was not even enough vegetation to hide it. The rocks offered the only choice, but it was also the perfect choice because from a distance the body would go undetected. What the bastard who did it hadn't counted on was young Nick, the wandering iPhone addict.

Nick appears to be okay. He's found a boulder to sit on and continues to occupy himself with his device.

'It says here that if someone is dead, he doesn't bleed because the heart has stopped pumping blood.'

And I thought he was in permanent text mode. 'Makes sense.'

'So that's why there's very little blood beyond the wound.'

I don't get it. 'He was dead when his throat was cut? Why would someone kill him and then slit his throat?'

Critical question that I don't have an answer for. Was the murderer's hate for his victim so strong that he couldn't resist one final vengeful act? Same question with the penis. A jealous lover out for revenge? Or maybe it was all a ploy to send the cops in the wrong direction when the body was finally discovered.

'It had to be that,' Nick says, his mind still on the lack of blood.

'We're assuming there were major blood vessels cut. Maybe not, maybe it was only his windpipe.'

'You mean his trachea.'

They don't call it a smartphone for nothing. 'The carotid and jugular are farther back, below the ears. It would have to have been a very wide cut to have a huge loss of blood.'

'Hey, look at this. You remember an NHL player named

Clint Malarchuk? Oh, gross!' He looks up at me, away from the screen.

Malarchuk—he was the goalie who had his throat slashed by a skate blade. Nick hands me the phone. There it is—video of him, his hand against his neck, a massive amount of his blood all over the ice.

'Nick, man, you don't need that.'

He gets out of YouTube, back to some other site. '1989. He was playing for the Buffalo Sabers. Listen to this.' He quotes from the screen: 'There was so much blood that eleven fans fainted, two more suffered heart attacks, and three players vomited on the ice.'

'Malarchuk thought he was going to die. But the team's trainer pinched off the blood vessel until the doctors got to work on him.'

'You're right,' Nick says. As if I don't know my hockey history.

I move off and retake a position at the crime scene. By this time the constable has completed her first round of photography. She's pallid, but still standing.

MacAvery turns his attention to the removal of the rocks partially covering the body. He is of the opinion that this is best undertaken prior to the arrival of the ambulance and reinforcements. Less confusion, less distraction during any subsequent picture-taking.

Possibly less embarrassment for the constable, who at any minute could faint and strike her head on the rocks.

'Gentlemen,' says MacAvery, turning to me and then Jean-Claude. 'I will be seeking your assistance.'

How good of the staff sergeant to include us. To buck regulations and place the eminent hand of the RCMP on our shoulders. The pressure to perform well is massive.

MacAvery has decided to assign each of the rocks covering

the body a number. In that way, he reveals, investigators will be able to keep track of what rock lay where before it was removed. He produces an indelible black marker and goes about the task, which, I will admit, requires a certain amount of physical (not to mention, arithmetical) dexterity.

When the job is complete, Constable Trottier is summoned to photograph his handiwork. Care must be taken that all numbered rocks and any exposed body parts are clearly in focus. The constable retreats to her previous location, even more pallid, but again remaining erect. Likely she is encouraged by my admiring nod.

MacAvery has designated an area, now suitably framed by yellow tape, to which the numbered rocks are to be relocated.

'Shall we begin? Brace yourself, this will not be a pleasant task.'

Onward. The choice of who will remove which rock is left to us. As might be expected, the slab covering much of the face is one of the least favoured, surpassed only by what Jean-Claude quietly refers to as 'the cock rock.'

His English is more nuanced than expected. Without discussing it, we seem to have jointly agreed to leave the two rocks in question to MacAvery. He, for his part, would seem to be leaving them for us. When we are down to only the two remaining, Jean-Claude and I step away from the body.

Except for the head and the member, it is fully exposed. Naked, lying on his side, the dead man would look to be of slightly less than average height. Slim, and even though his flesh bears the imprint of the rock, he would appear to have been in good shape.

Age? That waits for the removal of the slab of rock. MacAvery finally takes charge of it, and what is revealed is surprisingly intact, as if the slab had been set gently on the fellow's face.

He's far from looking his best, but even so, it is easily concluded that he was a handsome lad, I would guess in his mid-20s. I'm no expert but I would place him as being South Asian. But drawing back, viewing the body as a whole, the repulsive ugliness of the scene cuts even deeper. A virile life snatched away, in such a cruel and savage manner. And when the final numbered rock is removed, his mangled manhood revealed in all its hideousness, there is a plaintive, morbid, collective groan.

The mutilation was nothing if not deliberate, nothing if not vindictive. Making a definite statement, that's one thing for certain.

There need to be more pictures taken, and the constable looks like she can barely contain her nausea. If MacAvery hasn't got the balls to take on the job, I'll do it, police regulations or no police regulations. I stare his way until he gets the message. Finally he takes the camera out of the queasy constable's hands and passes it to me. 'Close-up and in focus, Mr. Synard.' Pervert.

I'll be the first to admit it's a crude and embarrassing business. Photographing dead body parts is an indelicate enterprise, to say the least. The head of a young man who made an abrupt and violent exit from this world fills the frame like nothing to which I have ever directed a lens. And then to reposition that lens to that same man's mashed meat, close-up and in desperate focus, is there any wonder that once the shutter is depressed, I lurch away. To my credit the puke lands nowhere near the yellow-taped rectangle. Damn beef jerky.

'Dad, you okay?'

I look up to see Nick running toward me. A widened palm forces him to a stop.

'Stay back where you were, Nick. Not for you to see.' The strands of vomit laced with saliva still clinging to my chin do nothing to placate him.

I wrap an arm around his shoulder and together we walk

off, mighty good buds, as if nothing out of the ordinary has taken place.

By the time the ambulance personnel and police re-enforcements arrive, the camera has been wiped clean and returned to Constable Trottier. They all looked at me with restrained pity. No one spoke of the incident. Wise choice.

MacAvery is suddenly in his element. He is exceptionally adept at telling other people what to do. Once the new round of revulsion to the dead and desecrated has played itself out, once they have all been briefed as to what exactly has taken place up to this point, then, finally, the job of removing the poor bastard onto the high-tech stretcher and off the Tablelands begins.

It's a delicate operation. MacAvery would like, to quote the staff sergeant, "to maintain, as much as possible, the posture of the victim, for the sake of the coroner's investigation." Which means, position him on the stretcher like he was on the ground. Obviously easier said than done.

They bugger it up of course. The victim looks worse on the stretcher than he did on the ground. A crumpled up, mutilated corpse that in all likelihood will look even worse by the time it is humped and bumped all the way down the mountain.

Tonight, back at the cabin where Nick and I are spending our last night before heading back to St. John's, solemnity fills the rooms. It has not been a good day. One we won't soon forget, and it worries me that the first time Nick personally experiences death, it is marked by such violence.

I try to set it in a context that will somehow make it easier for him. 'I'm willing to bet this is the first time there has ever been a murder in the Park.'

Right away he's on the Internet. He comes up short. Only

the report of someone missing years ago, empty car discovered within the park boundary, person still not found.
It does nothing to calm him. 'Nick, pal, these things happen. There is a lot of rough stuff in the world, and going through life you're bound to encounter it. Hopefully from a distance. But in this case we weren't so lucky.'

He's tight to me on the sofa. Just when I think he's growing up, cutting the ties a bit more every day, the unimaginable comes along and he needs me more than ever. After a while he goes off to bed, but within a half hour he's back again.

'I can't sleep.'

I move to one end of the sofa with my book. Nick grabs a blanket and curls up on the remaining part, his head on a pillow propped against my leg. I hold the book in one hand while the other strokes the top of his head, through hair that he regularly styles with some expensive paste or other, that now is limp and out of sorts.

It's odd that I should be reading *Hamlet*. I'm not in the habit of reading Shakespeare, or any plays for that matter. It came from having seen Benedict Cumberbatch as Hamlet in the National Theatre production a few days ago, broadcast from the Barbican Theatre in London to cinemas around the world. His performance blew me away.

I studied *Hamlet* in university. Had forgotten most of it, but was surprised by how much came back to me in the theatre. The classic lines of course—'to be or not to be,' 'something rotten in the state of Denmark,' 'neither a borrower nor a lender be,' 'what a piece of work is a man!'—but so much more that seemed buried deep inside my viscera, waiting to resurface.

Reading the play about the Prince of Denmark became the perfect route to a Danish whisky I had recently acquired. Yes, *Danish* whisky. Not that I'm surprised anymore by where in the world whisky distilleries are popping up.

When I'm not trying to make a living, I spend a day or so a month writing a whisky blog. Of course there are hundreds of people out there doing the same thing. They all have an angle. This is mine: I combine the reading of a book with the drinking of a whisky that somehow relates to it. Then jabber on about them both, combine it with a few pictures, and *voilà*, I'm a certified whisky blogger. Who gets, on average, four, maybe five hits a day. But hey, they do add up. Over 2500 since I started. From all over the world. One day this week, hits from Australia, the Philippines, the U.S., Norway, and Brazil. (It's the broad multinational ramifications of what I do that keeps me going month after month.)

In a moment of whisky-induced inspiration I titled the blog *Distill My Reading Heart!* Yes, way too cool.

So it's me working my way through Act Two, into the so-called "fishmonger scene," while Nick dozes next to me. It's one of my favourite bits of the play, when Hamlet dubs Polonius a fishmonger, and we don't know whether Hamlet is mad, or just pretending, putting one over on Polonius. Cumberbatch nails it, but I actually like David Tennant's take on it even more.

The skinny Scot did it in 2009 for BBC television. A fiercely agile performance, and it's all there for the viewing on YouTube. I'm always amazed what pops up on the Internet when you're not looking.

Here I am, with the Royal Shakespeare Company's annotated edition of *Hamlet*, lubricated by whisky from Distilleriet Braunstein, boosted further by another website I lucked into, one that splices together a sequence of seventeen different versions of the fishmonger scene, from Kenneth Branagh, Mel Gibson, Ethan Hawke even!, back to Derek Jacobi (now, another favourite), all the way back to Richard Burton and Laurence Olivier. Amazing compilation. Who knew?

'Whataya watching?'

He's not asleep after all. When I mention David Tennant he springs to life. 'Really? I love Doctor Who.'

One of Tennant's other claims to fame. Played the Doctor in three series and a bunch of specials.

I'd have thought that getting a thirteen-year-old hooked on *Hamlet* would be beyond my skill set. It helps that the production is in modern dress and Hamlet runs around barefoot and in a t-shirt much of the time. And when I play the Tennant fishmonger bit, with Tennant slithering about the stage and screwing up his face to taunt Polonius, Nick figures he could be watching Monty Python, which we do together a lot.

So he wants to see the whole thing. And so there you go. Three hours of *Hamlet*, me and the book helping him through the dialogue when the 400-year-old jargon gets the better of him, and me. Watching *Hamlet* turns into a stress-buster for both of us. Despite the multiple murders. Or maybe because of them.

When Hamlet mistakenly kills Polonius and indifferently declares he'll "lug the guts into the neighbour room," Nick looks at me, not sure if he should find it funny. I chuckle to give him permission to do the same. As if Shakespeare had written the line to give us both the opportunity to be our droll selves again.

At that point in the play you really have to think hard on whether Hamlet has lost it completely. And, if not insane, then what is a man that he would draw the dagger or thrust the rapier with the intention of bringing whoever lurks about the room to his final end.

What drove the killer who walked about the Tablelands? What drove someone to such a heinous crime? Was the butcher mad? I'm thinking too methodical to be mad.

What a piece of work is a man indeed.

3

AS AGREED TO, I stop in at the cop station in Rocky Harbour before driving back across the island to St. John's. The fresh, early morning light filters across the waters of Bonne Bay, and onto the mountains, but I've no mind for scenery.

Nick stays in the car while I check things out inside the station. Constable Trottier is sitting behind a desk, her workday well under way. A murder hangs in the air, all too far from a common circumstance. She seems to have recovered overnight, however, more or less. The tension, if not gone, has at least dissipated to a manageable level. She greets me with a formal and measured smile. A bit more relaxed, she could so easily set ablaze a man's heart.

'Good morning.'

'Good morning, Natasha.'

Her welcome tightens. Revealing her first name, she now recognizes, was a mistake. A slip-up in an unguarded moment, a hand unnecessarily extended. More than likely a weakness left over from her rural upbringing.

'Staff Sergeant MacAvery not around?'

I tried to avoid any whiff of hope in my voice.

'He's on his way back from Deer Lake. The body was put

in an ambulance for St. John's, for examination by a forensic pathologist. Western Memorial couldn't handle it.'

That would be the regional hospital in Corner Brook. 'I would have thought they'd have flown him in.'

'No rush. He's dead after all.'

I anticipated slightly more compassion. She has morphed into the epitome of the efficient police officer. Taking her cue, my tone becomes somewhat more professional, placing front and centre my career move to private detective. Constable Trottier is in need of a gentle reminder that we are on a comparable footing.

'I assume that the body has been identified, that some evidence turned up.' A slight falsehood, to test her willingness to cooperate. When we left with the body to make our way down the Tablelands, two extra officers were about to scour the site. I don't expect they found much, not if the killer had two clues.

'I'm not at liberty to disclose that. Police confidentiality, Mr. Synard.'

An attempt to cut me off at the knees. Not likely, Constable Trottier.

'Really? Wouldn't it be in the best interest of the RCMP to share a few details, in case they trigger some additional information? I did encounter several individuals during our climb up, as well as on our way down. I have a good memory for clothes. Perhaps the killer left...'

'I suggest you raise your concerns with Staff Sergeant MacAvery when he arrives.'

'I'm thinking they do things differently in Saskatchewan.'

She stares at me. I maintain eye contact with a hint of jest, which throws her off her game for the moment.

'What exactly are you talking about?'

'Taking the public into your confidence. You never know where it might lead. For example, if you were to say to me "the police have found what appears to be a single glove next to rocks that seem to have been slightly disturbed," then I might say, oh, I recall passing someone on my way up the mountain, someone heading down and wearing only one glove. I thought it strange at the time, and when I looked at him more closely I noticed…'

'There is no glove, Mr. Synard.'

'Let's drop the "Mister," shall we. Call me Sebastian.'

An impulsive moment. One that doesn't go over particularly well.

'I see…' She shuffles through some papers. '…that you recently turned fifty, Mr. Synard. That would make me less than half your age. I have no interest in referring to you as Sebastian. And if you think that by being chummy with me you will gain access to confidential information, then I'm afraid you're mistaken.'

Well now, aren't we the combative constable. 'I guess I don't understand how it works on the Prairies after all. So much open space. Minds must roam a bit too wide for me.'

'I suggest you take a seat, Mr. Synard.'

I might just do that. I might just sit down in one of the two uncomfortable chairs in the reception area and look through a brilliant piece of police literature titled *Crime Prevention through Environmental Design*. Yes, I prefer being bored out of my skull reading a pamphlet to trying to engage the constable in further conversation.

Nick shows up, wondering what's taking me so long.

'Good morning, Nick,' says the constable. Suddenly the chameleon, smiling warmly. 'I like your t-shirt.'

'Thanks.'

'I like their music.'

'Cool.'

Cool? Really? Who calls their band Mercy, the Sexton?

'Too bad they broke up,' says the constable.

'Yeah,' says Nick. 'Like really cool.'

Like it's really cool to be into obscure bands that no longer exist?

It suddenly occurs to me that the constable, mature woman that she is, is closer in age to my son than she is to me. A lot closer.

I never thought it would be a relief to see MacAvery.

The additional vehicle in the parking lot has prepared him for another unconventional day at the cop station. He turns as he comes through the door, correct in his assumption that the chairs are occupied.

I politely place the pamphlet back with the thick pile of others just like it and stand to greet the staff sergeant. 'A busy start to the day I hear. The body on its way to the capital city? Must be a grim gig for the ambulance driver. Not many murder victims to be had in this part of the world.'

He glances over at the constable, who fails to make eye contact. 'No problems, Mr. Synard. Everything went according to plan.'

'It's a shame the corpse couldn't have been examined right away. I understand your chap in Corner Brook couldn't handle it.'

He glances at the constable a second time, with no more success.

'From my experience, the sooner the better. The forensic boys prefer them fresh.'

'You did well on your exam, Mr. Synard.'

I stare blankly. He doesn't deserve anything more.

'Your private investigator certification, you did well? You did go the route of proper training? Hands-on, not one of those quick online jobs?'

'As a matter of fact, no, it wasn't particularly quick. Thank you for asking.'

Prick. Six six-week courses. Online or not, they were intense. 'I'm heading into St. John's. You asked me to stop by.' To state the obvious.

The next thing we know, Nick and I are alone in a room with a laptop and printer and not much else, typing up a joint statement on the discovery of the body and what followed. Nick dictates, I put it in standard English, adding my bit. It doesn't take long. Print, date, and sign.

'Please make sure Constable Trottier has your complete contact information,' MacAvery says, having given the statement a quick read. 'I'll be in touch, as needed.'

That's it? We're out of the picture. Job done.

May need you again, may not. See you in court, if it ever comes to that. Off you go. Drive safely. Watch out for moose. And, by the way, all information about the crime scene remains strictly confidential until such time as it is made public by the police.

MacAvery takes me aside after the unsmiling constable has her info and I'm about to trail Nick out the door. 'You may want to consider trauma counselling for the young fellow. And for yourself, if I were you.'

How compassionate. And here I was thinking the RCMP was all about getting their man.

'These things can take their toll,' he adds.

Should I weep now, or vomit when I go outside?

'Good-bye, Constable. Have a highly rewarding day. And the same to you, Staff Sergeant.'

I don't look back. I'm off the parking lot as fast as I can manage, bearing in mind it's RCMP property. No such holdback when I get on the main road.

'Dad, slow down.'

The kid's right, of course. We have eight hours of driving ahead of us. I take a deep breath and ease back to the speed limit.

A good portion of those eight hours is spent solidifying the notion that I'm not willing to fade out of the picture so easily. We are, after all, heading straight to the city where the dead body is being held, about to undergo a forensic assessment.

St. John's has its own police force, the RNC, the Royal Newfoundland Constabulary. (Or, more affectionately, the Constab.) The investigation, however, remains in the hands of the RCMP, which has a Major Crime Unit at its detachment in the capital city. Being thoroughly versed in the province's police structure, I do know that the RCMP buddies up with the RNC as needed. Depending on the scope of the crime, the Mounties will call on the Constab to help rev up an investigation.

I just happen to have become well acquainted with said Constab in the course of other employment I engage in from time to time, that of tour guide. I'm at the stage of my life (having quit teaching prematurely and without a pension for the foreseeable future) of having to make money where the opportunity presents itself.

By luck (bad in this case, but still luck) I have a good "in" with the RNC. Olsen. Inspector F. Olsen (F for Frederick, but only when I'm in a good mood). The cop who just happens to share living space with my ex-wife, Samantha. Mother of Nick, the kid sitting next to me in the car, playing a game on his iPad.

The aforementioned living space includes a well-appointed bedroom, painted and wallpapered by my very own hand. They say wallpapering together is the test of a relationship. Perhaps not surprisingly then, by the end of our last attempt at affixing a few rolls, Samantha and I were at each other's throats.

Regarding Olsen, all is fiendishly complicated. Samantha apparently loves him, Nick used to hate him but has moderated his attitude slightly, and I'm caught somewhere in the middle. If strong-armed I will admit that Olsen is a good cop. He did have occasion to help save my ass, and he has a taste for Scotch—all working in his favour. Our animosity has cooled to the point of civil conversation. Whether or not he'll be willing to do me a favour and facilitate access to the autopsy report is an open question. I'm willing to give him the benefit of the doubt.

'Nick, pal, you're missing out on some beautiful scenery.' He grunts his disinterest. I've thrown him some slack, and let him game-out as much as he wants. He needs diversion from all that's happened. In any case, before long his battery will go dead, and since I don't have a car charger for the iPad, he'll eventually end up with his fair share of scenery.

While he's gaming I at least get to have my choice of radio stations. Which means CBC One or Two. Nick pays no mind to what he terms "boring old CBC." Until the news broadcast breaks the flow of his concentration.

'Hey, that's us.'

Referring to "the two hikers who discovered the body." Being "unavailable for comment" means some reporter must have tried but had no way of knowing how to get in touch with us. I have no desire to have our names ricocheting around the airwaves. It would not be good for Nick. Or, for that matter, my tour-guide business.

My cell phone, lying in the cup holder between the seats, rings.

'Get that, Nick. It's probably your mother wondering when we're getting back.'

'Nope, not Mom,' he says, glancing at the incoming number. 'Hello.' Before checking with me. 'No, this is his son. He's driving.' Nick puts the phone out of voice range, whispering, 'It's some guy from the CBC, he wants to talk to me.'

Fuck. 'No. Absolutely not.'

Nick into the phone: 'My father says no, absolutely not.' Pause. He turns to me again, this time not bothering to move the phone from his ear. 'What's a good time to reach you?'

Never. 'Tell him I'll call back. When it's convenient.'

Which will not be anytime soon. How the hell did they get my number?

The phone rings again. This time it's Samantha.

'Hi, Mom.' Pause. 'Yeah, I know. They called. No, we're not in any trouble.'

End of guessing where CBC got the friggin number.

'Can I tell her?'

The shoulder of the highway is wide enough to pull over. I put my hand out for the phone and take a deep breath. Nick shrugs.

'Hi, Sam.' It's automatic, calling her Sam, even though she says she hates it. Suddenly, once divorce proceedings started, she hates it. Too "familiar." Now reserved for Olsen, no doubt.

A steady barrage of questions, which I attempt to answer one by one, remaining calm and somewhat collected. I downplay it as much as I can, ignoring the admonishment, much repeated, that I should have called earlier.

'He's fine.' Followed by agitated disagreement at the other end of the phone. 'You don't have to tell me it was a traumatic experience.' Further agitation. 'Maybe we all need counselling.' Wrong thing to have said.

Normally I would hold the phone away from my ear until she finishes, but that would not be something Nick needs to witness. For his sake, I work hard at maintaining the façade of an amicable relationship between his parents.

Finally there's a pause in the one-sided conversation. 'I will, Samantha, I'll make sure he calls as soon as we get back. You'll see him tomorrow.' Pause. 'I'll do my best.' A discreet roll of my eyes. 'Here's Nick. I have to get back on the road.'

Nick manages to fit in more words, enough, it would appear, to reassure her he's not suffering from PTSD.

I shouldn't be flippant. It happens.

We stop at Gander, which is about halfway across the island, to gas up and for something to eat. I was born and raised in Gander. My parents are both dead now; the family home has been sold, although I still have a sister who lives here. We won't go visit my sister. A story better avoided.

Gander, a town of 12,000, has become famous. In the hours after 9-11 it took in 7,000 airline passengers from Europe left stranded when the U.S. closed its air space. The story of the townspeople's incredible hospitality landed on Broadway and put Gander on the map.

Actually it's always been on the map. When I was growing up, Gander was known as the "Crossroads of the World." Because it was *the* refuelling stop for airlines flying between Europe and North America, before they could do it in one shot and didn't need Gander anymore. Shame. It has an extraordinary 1950s international departure lounge, one of the finest Modernist rooms anywhere—from the Mondrian-like terrazzo flooring to the cutting-edge furniture to the sweep of a Kenneth Lochhead mural that runs almost the entire length of one wall.

'Frank Sinatra, Kissinger, Yassar Arafat, they all stopped here.' Doesn't raise a teenage eyebrow. 'Nelson Mandela, Elizabeth Taylor, Marlene Dietrich, Castro, the Beatles.'

'The Beatles, really?'

'What do they teach you in school these days?' As if I don't know, having been a Social Studies teacher for all of my aborted career. They teach them History when and where there's room on the timetable after Science and Math have sucked up the prime spots. Don't get me started.

We're standing in the glassed-in viewing area that overlooks the lounge. Of course we can't actually set foot inside the lounge anymore. 'I remember hanging out here when I was your age.

No security then. You could come and go as you please. Hang out, drink pineapple Fanta, and people watch.'

'Wow.' Dripping sarcasm. 'One cool dude. In the day.'

'Laugh if you want. Bet you've never seen Arnold Schwarzenegger, *dude*.'

Knew that would fire up his brain cells. Nick would be all about weight training if he had his way. Last year his mother gave into his whining and bought him weights and a bench, never thinking for one second what damage it can do to a kid's bones and muscles. I wasn't long putting a stop to it.

'You saw Arnold Schwarzenegger?'

'Didn't really. But he was here. We definitely did see Bob Hope.'

It rings no bells.

Still, it's good for Nick to experience a bit of my growing up. The truth is, despite living in the "Crossroads of the World," I couldn't wait to get out. Couldn't wait to finish high school and race off to university. My parents were happy enough to see me go. They were of a generation that struggled through an education system so sub-standard that it encouraged people to quit and go out to work, which for my father was cod-fishing with his father, out from a place called Salvage. A hard life and little chance of ever making a living any other way.

The old man struck it lucky. The town of Gander grew up out of nothing in the early days of transatlantic aviation, then boomed during WWII and for years after, so much so that it gathered in young men and their families from all over the island. My newly married parents moved to Gander, as they always liked to remember, the day in 1959 that Queen Elizabeth II arrived to open the newly built terminal. By the time I came along, Dad was well into his new job with Gander Aviation, and we had just moved into a new house on Lindbergh Road.

I drive by the house on our way back to the highway, slowing down enough to see it hasn't changed much. New siding, trees a lot bigger, that's about all. Plenty of street hockey played in front of that house.

'A lot of the streets are named after aviators—Earhart, Rickenbacker, Bishop,' I tell Nick. 'Some not so famous.'

'Not so famous. Like who?' He's testing me.

'Like Louise Sacchi.' I'm surprised I can pull up her name after all those years, since doing the project in junior high. Probably because it's a bit of an odd name, and the fact she was female. 'She ferried planes, flew solo across the Atlantic and the Pacific over 300 times, a record. She crashed once, in the middle of winter, just after taking off from Gander. Came out of it alive. One very tough bird.'

'Doesn't Aunt Melissa live on Sacchi?'

Right, that's why. Speaking of tough birds.

'Aren't we going to stop by and see her?'

'She's probably not home.'

He knows enough not to take it any further. He knows my sister and I haven't been getting along for years, since our widower father took sick and she ended up looking out to him, doing what needed to be done. I stayed away, until it was time to collect half the inheritance.

I admit now I was an ass. A much-resented ass. Things were starting to fall apart with Samantha at the time. That's how I justified it.

I don't need more complications in my life, but it doesn't stop me from turning in the opposite direction from the highway and rerouting through several streets until I reach Sacchi.

Nick doesn't ask. He's perceptive, he knows my mind is churning. Counterclockwise, running with a sudden urge, even though what I am about to do will likely only make it worse between myself and Melissa. Worse, not better as is my hope once I stop the car next to the sidewalk in front of her house.

'You want to come in with me?'

Don't want him thinking he's along to diffuse a potential scene. Because she's less likely to let loose yet again when Nick is standing next to me.

Her car is in the driveway. I'm not surprised. She's a real estate agent and often works from home. In fact she's the one who sold the family property, something which made a nasty situation nastier. She declined the commission even though I told her she should take it. Even suggesting it was another thorn, a further mark against me, not that our relationship wasn't already on the skids by then.

Her surprise is obvious, her indecision about what reaction she should offer up to us goes on too long. Finally she widens the door and invites us inside. Nick steps quickly ahead of me, seemingly to put himself in the front line. He makes a motion to hug her, very unlike him, and she has no choice but to respond in kind. Her quarrel is not with her nephew. In fact, she always liked Nick, never fails to remember his birthday and Christmas.

A hug for me will not be in the cards, and I know better than to try.

'This is a surprise,' she says, as neutral as she is able to make it.

'Can't stop long.' Let's make that clear up front. Let's put a measure on the discomfort she will have to endure.

I explain what we've been up to over the past few days, only bringing in the murder at the end.

'I heard it on the news. You were the two who found him? Really?'

Bizarre as it is, the anxiety level dissipates, somewhat. Something greater than all of us has grabbed the attention, outweighing the angst.

And that's the most of it really. We don't stay long. We leave as we came in, no mention of the rift between us, no acknowledgment of past mistrust. So what was my intent? If there is going to be reconciliation of any sort there had to be a first step. The longer the silence, the more bitter the bile. As my father would say.

Melissa is married to Merle. I haven't seen him lately, of course, but before all this sibling crap, Merle and I got along pretty well. Much better than I did with Melissa. Drank a good few beers together and even went off salmon fishing a couple of times. Me with my single malt, Merle with his Old Sam.

It's a guy thing. Men don't build up grudges the way women do. (Another in my vast arsenal of communal observations.)

Melissa and Merle don't have kids. Not sure the reason behind it, but I can't imagine they wouldn't have wanted at least one. Maybe a fertility issue. Why they wouldn't have adopted, who knows. It is not something we ever discussed. And certainly won't now.

An only child and it ends up a mess. Families are strange creatures.

Nick and I don't say much for the next hour or so. Just before the island's other national park—Terra Nova—we pass the turn-off to the Eastport Peninsula, once home to the parental Synard. As a kid I spent a lot of summer holidays there, on the beaches. Nick the same. Family time, which I miss actually.

Samantha, Nick, and I, from the time he was a toddler. It was the best of the marriage—white sand, beach chairs, bucket and shovel, Swedish mysteries, ice-packed jar of Hendrick's gin and tonic. Samantha as tantalizing as she was during the honeymoon in Antigua. The summer easing out the tensions of teaching. We could smile at each other then and never think it was anything but spontaneous.

There's a news update coming from the car radio that suddenly shifts my headspace.

'The victim has been identified as Simón Torres, twenty-six, originally from Mexico. Mr. Torres was a graduate student in Earth Sciences at Memorial University, and had been in Newfoundland for only six weeks.'

The mutilated corpse has suddenly become a real person.

4

LET'S JUST SAY I have an acquaintance in the Department of Earth Sciences of Memorial University. Living in a small city like St. John's, you always know someone who knows someone. It's Newfoundland after all.

He's the husband of Claire, who is a good friend of Samantha. For me, husband of a friend now once removed, so to speak. Nevertheless, I think he still falls safely in the acquaintance category.

His name is Blane McKay. Blane and the fiercely loyal (word has it) Claire came to dinner several times, when Samantha and I were still having people to dinner, when dinner together was something we still did. That would make it at least six months before the split, which means it's probably been three years since I last conversed with Blane. If I recall correctly, at the time it was a lot of barbecue/Netflix talk. I wasn't much into geology. Not like I am now, given that I have to be, given that it's a necessity if you're a tour guide in a place world-renowned for its geological features (i.e., Newfoundland; i.e., the Rock).

I find Blane's contact info in the university's online directory. I give him a nonchalant ring. He answers right away, which likely means he's at his office desk. He's surprised to hear from me, as you would expect. He's distinctly less chummy than I remember. He does a hopelessly poor job of disguising the edge of distrust in his voice. No doubt a result of getting the divorce story through Claire, unsullied by the truth.

I press ahead. 'Blane, Nick and I are the hikers who discovered the body of Simón Torres on the Tablelands.'

'Really?' His tone changes. Suddenly he perks.

'Indeed. It was hellish for both of us. The way the throat was slashed.'

'What?' Perking even higher.

He had no idea about the throat, as I suspected. 'That's confidential, by the way. The cops have yet to make it public.'

Having taken him into my confidence, I feel myself sliding firmly into the driver's seat.

'Good God.'

While I have him at his most pliable, I make my pitch. 'As a friend, Blane, I'd like to talk to you. The RCMP is moving ahead on this, but as someone central to the investigation, I need to give them any help I can.' Not strictly police procedure, but given that he's a geology professor, he is not likely to question it.

'What help exactly?'

Let's not get technical, Blane.

'I'd like to meet you at your office. Today if possible. It's urgent, as you can imagine.'

'I have a class at 11. A meeting at 3:30.'

'1:30 then. I'll be there at 1:30. It shouldn't take long.'

He doesn't say yes, but doesn't say no.

'Good. See you then.' I go straight to hang up.

His office is rather less impressive than I imagined. After all, according to my calculations, he's been a tenured professor for a good twenty years. I take my clue from the relic of a name plaque imbedded in the door, a yellowed Peanuts cartoon strip doing its best to remain taped above it. It features Snoopy's older brother Spike sitting next to a rock in a desert, wondering, "Do you find that being a rock is boring?"

Truly. I knock gently but assertively.

'Come in.' Sounding like an automated response, as if it's another of his students who's come knocking. He's not about to make the effort of walking to the door.

He does stretch his hand forward, over his desk. 'Take a seat.'

I gently close the door behind me. The office is small, with most of the walls taken up with bookcases. But it does have a window, if not much of a view. I take note of what the professor has on the wall space not given over to books. I expected a tired poster on igneous rocks. Instead, my eyes fall on one of those inspirational groaners I remember as being hopelessly common in school corridors. There's a big cloud-strewn blue sky above a boulder-laden shoreline, imprinted with: "Courage is what it takes to stand up and speak; courage is also what it takes to sit down and listen. –Winston S. Churchill."

The professor has his boundaries. All who enter pissed off at their mark on the last exam take note.

I am not so readily intimidated. 'How have you been, Blane? The world still treating you well?'

'I have no complaints.'

I was hoping for some. Sharing in misery is a proven equalizer. I take another route. 'How's Claire? Still teaching power yoga?'

'Let's get to the point, Sebastian. When the cops say "foul play is suspected" they're talking murder. Correct?'

Blane never did strike me as a patient man. 'It was a grisly scene, the slashed throat and all. You would not have wanted to be the one to discover him.'

He shakes his head, a grimace set into his face. 'It has hit the department very hard.' A definite softening.

'What brought him to Newfoundland? I wouldn't think you get many students from Mexico.'

'He just finished up his master's program at the University of Texas. His thesis was brilliant. He wanted out of the States. You hear that a lot lately.'

'Highly recommended?' Considering he was still in his mid-twenties.

'We were very lucky to get him. Of course, it helped that his work was in geophysics and tectonics.'

'Which explains why he was on the Tablelands.'

I am stating the obvious. The professor exhibits unmistakable signs of losing patience.

'Was he making friends? Did he have a girlfriend?'

'How would I know? He was a grad student. We advise them. We're not their bosom buddies.'

'So you only saw him on campus?'

He hesitates. 'We had all the new grad students over to the house last week. For drinks and conversation. A goodwill gesture. Claire's idea. We do it every year.'

'So you interacted with him on a social level.'

'Listen, Synard, what is this? I'm being interrogated?'

'Interrogated? You misunderstand, Blane. The more we know about Simón Torres, the better. This is a murder investigation.'

He stares intently at me. 'Do the police know what you're on about? These questions of yours—who are they really for?'

It appears it would not be in my best interest to lie. 'Myself. They're for myself.'

Blank shakes his head. A grin is beginning to take shape.

'Murder is not amusing, Blane. And it just so happens that the father of the person who first discovered the murdered grad student is a private investigator.'

The grin is now fully formed. 'You, Sebastian? Are you making this up?'

'I fail to see the humour. So should you.'

There is no point in continuing. I leave the office with a caution. 'I'll be back in touch, Blane. I suggest we go for coffee. When you're in a more judicious frame of mind. In the meantime I'll go ahead and arrange a meeting with the head of the department.' I close the door pointedly behind me.

There's a student outside, about to knock. He looks like the type easily intimidated by Churchill.

I leave setting up a meeting with the department head until later. I need alone time, strategic planning time. Well, me and the mutt.

Fifteen-pound (at last weigh-in) Gaffer appears to have thrived during his time with Jeremy. If extra poundage is thriving. He returned home thinking himself deserving of as much food as he got when he was away. 'Sorry, pal, I'm not keen on overweight poodle-Maltese crosses.'

Maltese cross. There's a joke to be had somewhere in that. But I'm tired, I have too much on my mind. I need a shot of whisky and my favourite chair.

Gaffer takes to my lap, resigned to the fact that ball-throwing and treat-tossing are out of the picture. I text Nick to see how he's doing. He's back with his mother, and it's likely she will keep him under wraps until the weekend. As Samantha saw it, traumatized sons need their mothers, first and foremost. There was no point in arguing.

To me he didn't appear particularly traumatized anymore. If I'm reading between the lines of his texts correctly, his discovery of the body caused his street cred to soar. I suspect it's a bit of a show. Samantha says he's not sleeping well. She arranged counselling without consulting me, not that I'm not in favour. But it would have been reasonable for me to have had a say in it. No point in forcing the issue, though.

Amazing what the Internet can yield, once you get past several Simón Torreses to find the one you're after. Past the super welterweight boxer from California. Past the surfer guy who found himself and is "learning to ride that inner wave of Spirit." And a guy who plays frisbee golf, sometimes called "frolf." No kidding. Who knew? It veered me off to an episode of Seinfeld when George decides to take up frolf. Love Seinfeld. Not so sure about frolf.

Once I got back on track, there was a lot to be discovered about the real, though recently deceased, Simón Torres. Through comprehensive investigative procedures, this is the additional information I have uncovered so far. Lived in grad accommodations in what is known as the Signal Hill Campus. Was due to present at a grad student symposium called "The Earth Moves Under My Feet." (Carole King would be pleased.) Presentation based on the master's thesis written for his previous degree program at University of Texas in Austin. (No one has yet found a way to take down his Facebook page and Instagram account. They do serve as a reminder of what an impressive fellow he was.) Already published in a prodigious scientific journal. Swam freestyle for the University of Texas Longhorns. Headed up the university's Association of Mexican Americans. Known to write poetry and make a mean guacamole. Six weeks in Newfoundland and already conducting tours at the Johnson Geo Centre, the acclaimed museum of Earth Science.

Just across from the Geo Centre is the university's Signal Hill Campus, perched on a hill overlooking St. John's Harbour and the city surrounding it. The sign calls it the "Emera Innovation Exchange." Sounds like academic jargon to me. I do know it has a conference centre, and on its upper floors, eighty-seven apartments to house grad students. Surely to God they have the most impressive views of any grad residence in Canada. Can't say I know for certain. Haven't been able to figure out a way to get in one, but I'm working on it.

The break comes when I slip into the opening session of the symposium, which is conveniently taking place at the conference centre of said Signal Hill Campus. Carole King plays discreetly in the background as the chairs fill up. There was the potential for a very upbeat gathering, but of course a pall has descended over the whole event. The students have lost one of their own. They have made the decision to proceed with the symposium and officially dedicate it to Simón.

Looking around, I do a rough count of fifty people, sitting at tables, drinking coffee, mishandling oversized muffins, as a prelude to the opening remarks. It would seem most of the faculty is here, including contrarian Blane. He doesn't notice me, and I'd rather keep it that way, for the moment at least.

The symposium begins soberly, with a tribute from someone I take to be a best friend, someone who reveals he lived two doors away from Simón. I jot down the fellow's name in my notebook—Yon Carlson. I check the printed program to be sure I got it right. Make that Jón Karlsson.

Jón is having a tough go of it. He chokes up several times, but eventually gets through to the end. The thought occurs to me that his relationship with Simón might have been more than platonic. At the very least, their first names have an odd congruence.

More grad students take to the podium, relating anecdotes that further endear the dead young man to the audience. Then it is the turn of his faculty advisor, speaking on behalf of the Department. It is obvious they are at a loss to understand why anyone would want to 'cut him down in the prime of life.' An unfortunate cliché, but then he had no way of knowing just how the deed was accomplished.

And finally a Professor Troy Foster from the University of Texas. The professor has apparently come to pay his respects on behalf of the Earth Sciences Department where Simón completed his undergraduate and master's degrees and where he had done the research for his award-winning paper. In fact, in tribute to Simón, Professor Foster will be presenting his former student's paper later in the symposium.

We all stand for a minute of silence, before a ten-minute break to allow everyone time to reorganize their minds to something that resembles an academic symposium. Life must go on, the cruelty of the world set aside for the time being.

Of course my own mind finds it impossible to make the switch. Not that "Taconic orogeny" and "magma mingling" are not fascinating in and of themselves. I'm tending to focus on the presenters and whether there is even the slightest hint that one of them had anything to do with the murder, or could at the very least provide some helpful leads. At the moment they are my entry point.

At lunch break I am on to it. I am still successful in remaining out of Blane's field of vision. My attention is directed at Jón Karlsson.

He is seated with two other students, having just half-filled his plate at the buffet table. His upset has played havoc with his appetite. Understandable. I half fill my own plate in solidarity and am about to walk to where the three are seated when I notice Professor Foster approaching the buffet table.

In size, he's a Texan. A strapping 6' 4 at least. It's tough to be unobtrusive given that frame, but he tries, in keeping with the somber mood pervading the room. I detect a generous academic, well-liked by his students.

I introduce myself, adding 'my son and I were the two people who found Simón on the Tablelands.' Rather abrupt in retrospect.

He is too taken aback to even extend his hand. His emotion shows itself in a curt response. 'Not too awful I hope.'

He hasn't been told. He doesn't need to go back to Texas any more upset than he already is. 'No,' I lie, and leave it at that. The man needs his space.

'Simón died at the top of his game,' he says, then turns and moves off.

Before Jón and the two others have a chance to notice a complete stranger standing expectantly in front of them, a plate in one hand, a fork in the other, I volunteer my name. 'Mind if I join you?'

It's caught them off guard. Before it turns any more awkward, I provide the necessary connection to Simón. One of the three finally speaks. 'I'm Katerina.' She extends her hand in the direction of an empty place at the table. 'Please.'

At this point they have no way of knowing my underlying investigative intentions. My look is that of someone about to offer his condolences, which of course I do.

Of the three, Jón is the most ill at ease. He moves his food about the plate with his fork, not bothering to bring any of it to his mouth. 'I heard you speak,' I tell him. 'You two were very good friends.'

He nods. 'We met when he arrived from Mexico, the first week of the semester. I volunteered to show him around the university. We hit it off.' Jón's voice rises, 'Why would anyone want to kill Simón, Mr. Synard?' He shakes his head and abandons his fork on the plate.

Katerina quickly interjects. 'It must have been a terrible shock, to discover him. I can't imagine.'

They have no clue, and it's not for me to give them any.

The third student is desperate to be part of the conversation. 'He was always a smart dresser. Was there blood all over his clothes?'

'There's no need, Mark.'

Jón's admonishment gives me license not to answer him, thankfully.

Katerina, the peacemaker, steps in. 'We all liked him, Mr. Synard. He was a great guy. Serious about his studies, but he had his fun side.'

'You might say that,' says Mark.

Jón gives him the eye. Mark has more to offer up, I suspect.

It's as good a time as any for the reveal. 'I also happen to be a private investigator.'

It takes a few moments to process.

'For real?' says Jón. 'Did you just happen to be one? Or did you decide to take it up after you discovered the body?'

His upset does nothing for his manners. I answer him calmly and directly, for the sake of the investigation. 'As luck would have it, Jón, I had completed my training last month. But I will be honest, this is my first real case.'

'As opposed to the not-so-real ones?' says Mark.

A PI must retain his professionalism and refrain from falling to the level of the person he is investigating. I look at each of them in turn. 'Let's just say I scored in the ninetieth percentile on the final exam.'

That puts an end to that.

'Who hired you?' It's the ever-subtle Mark again.

'I'm afraid I'm not at liberty to say.' No lie there.

A quick change of focus is in order.

'I am sure all of you, as much as I, want a resolution to this very unfortunate incident. Make no mistake, it was murder, and a rather grisly one at that.'

Katerina winces, Mark's teeth lock together, Jón stiffens. I hadn't meant to, but it would have come out in due course. They needed a jolt of reality.

'With your help, I would like to convene a meeting of Simón's grad student friends, to see if, as a group, we might be able to come up with some clues, any clues, that could help with the case.'

'Isn't that the job of the police?'

I was waiting for that. 'Of course, but there's a lot to be said for a second pair of eyes. We all want a resolution to this. The police and I share the same goal, as do you I am sure.' A short pause. 'I assume you are all staying upstairs in the grad accommodations?'

All three nod, in something of a disjointed chain reaction.

'And I assume there is a common lounge area. How about Sunday? How about you pass the word to the other students and we convene in the morning, say 10:30? Not too early I hope.'

Another question posed. Another answer expected. Built around non-threatening language. A common investigative technique. Simple procedure for the ninetieth percentile.

They look at each other. I am waiting for one positive response, to start the ball rolling.

'I'm good with 10:30,' says Mark. He provides me with his cell number. I'll need to contact someone with elevator access.

Katerina shrugs. 'Fine with me…I guess.'

That leaves Jón. Why am I not surprised?

'Where do you call home, Jón?'

It's nothing he's expecting. Finally he tells me. 'Iceland.'

It's deserving of the Newfoundland head nod. Unique to Newfoundland, a cultural aberration, the physical equivalent of "good on ya." It combines a quick twist of the head and a wink. Foreigners generally haven't a clue what to make of it, so I'm taking my chances with Jón.

'Thanks,' he says, without batting an eye, so to speak. Really? He's obviously been getting around since he's been here.

I turn to Katerina.

'Germany.' She smiles and does a hopelessly bad version of the head nod. What is this?

I look at Mark, wondering what's coming next.

'Nippers Harbour.'
That's it?
He grins. 'I've been teaching them.' Then suddenly he turns solemn. 'Simón had it down pat.' He starts to choke-up. 'The poor bastard.'
'You all bring your own take on the world. You see things differently, just as Simón did, coming from Mexico. That's what I'm after—diverse cultural perspectives, so maybe, just maybe, they will trigger something you noticed in Simón's behaviour that can help solve this hideous crime.'
Jón is not left with much choice. He'll be there.

I decide to take the day to relax, refocus, and rebuild my strategy. The occasional dram of Lagavulin helps.
I wake suddenly when Gaffer jumps abruptly from my lap and races to the front door. I upright the La-Z-Boy.
It's Nick. 'Hey, pal.'
It's Saturday. He should be chilled. He should be all over Gaffer, who keeps jumping for attention. He's not. He's agitated.
'What's up?'
'Mom. She's driving me nuts.'
'I'm sure you're overstating it.'
'You don't have to live with her.'
I did, for a good chunk of my adult life. That quip, however, must be stifled.
'What's the problem?' I try being casual.
He clams up.
'I can't help if you won't tell me.'
'She wants me to see a psychiatrist. Thinks I need medication to help me sleep.'
'How is your sleep?'
'Not great,' he admits. 'But getting better. I'm seeing a counsellor. I'm not traumatized, if that's what she thinks.'

'You did go through a very messy experience.'
'I'm getting over it. It takes time.'
Self-diagnosis from a thirteen-year-old.
'Whose side you on?' he says.
Here we go. 'I'm not on anyone's side.'
His mother could be right. Knowing Samantha, she knows she's right.
'Where's boyfriend in all this? He's had plenty of experience with trauma. He should have some credible advice.' That would be boyfriend Frederick.
'He's not involved,' Nick says. 'He knows better.'
I won't go there. 'Can you bargain for time? Ask your mother if she'll give you a week before she takes any action.'
He shrugs.
'It's worth a try.'
'Maybe.'
Maybe is as good as it gets when the teenage mind is involved. I leave it at that.
Nick's mood softens somewhat, what with Gaffer refusing to take "no" for an answer to all his attempts at getting Nick's attention.
'He could use a walk.'
'I guess so.'
In case he doesn't remember, Nick is the reason Gaffer shares the house with me. He was desperate for a dog and worked past Samantha's display of logic as to why there couldn't be one in their domicile (both of them gone all day, *et cetera, et cetera*), until I gave in (the argument being that I have more flexible hours) and the mutt made the journey from the SPCA to my humbler digs. On the understanding, I will add, that Nick would share in the chores needed to keep Gaffer exercised, groomed, and well fed.
Usually it's not an issue. But today Nick is ambivalent. I have

faith in Gaffer. He'll wear him down.

And sure enough, when the two return to the house, Nick has brightened and is bursting to tell me what happened in Bannerman Park. 'You know that miniature schnauzer he despises?'

I do indeed. Any encounter between the two is never any less than a raging bark-fest.

'His name is Bingo, by the way. Can you believe it? Very sad. Very sad. No wonder the dog has a complex.' Nick is just getting started. He's good at working up a story. 'So I'm walking along with Gaffer, minding my own business, like you would, when Satan-on-four-paws breaks away from his owner and comes barrelling across the grass, fire in his eyes. His owner is yelling, "Bingo! Bingo, get back here!" Like hell he's going to go back. Suddenly Gaffer sees him and starts straining at the lead, barking like he's ready to tear Bingo limb from limb. I was tempted. I tell you, I was tempted.'

'Gaffer would have come out the loser.' Gaffer is sitting at our feet, peering up with a quizzical look, prepared to defend himself if he could talk.

'That's what I thought. So I snapped him up in my arms. Just in time, too. Bingo-brain's teeth almost grazed his fur.'

'What about the owner?'

'She finally made it across the field, waving her cane at Bingo.'

I like to think I am raising a boy with some measure of compassion. I prompt him. 'You got to hand it to the woman. Bingo must be a tough mutt to keep under control.'

'Yeah. Maybe,' he says. He doesn't shrug. That's positive.

'The dogs could learn to get along,' I suggest. 'They just need to sniff each other out.'

'That I doubt. Bingo would go right for the jugular.'

Only after the fact does he think about what he said. There

are dog jugulars, and then there are human jugulars. Violence seems to be coming at him from every angle.

Sometimes the less said the better.

Instead we cook supper together. Definitely not red meat. Something vegetarian. A pasta something or other. It's food bonding time again. Father, son, dog, pasta.

The morning sees me in eager mode. I've done my homework. Revisited my course sections on interviewing techniques. Drawn up a list of possible questions. Edited the questions so they will elicit the most revealing answers. Had another, particularly caffeine-stiff, coffee.

It will take a while to get my sea legs, just as it did with the tour guiding business. I see this as off-season employment, something to keep the mind up and running between tourist seasons. It just so happens that the first case fell into my lap unsolicited. A fortunate break, if I look at it that way. Prime chance to get the feet wet.

Out of the car at the Signal Hill Campus, I phone ahead to Mark, who meets me in the lobby.

He shakes my hand and yawns at the same time. 'Sorry. Up late. You know.'

I do. My own university career had its share of sleep deprivation.

With his access card in hand, he leads me to the elevator, and in due course into the student lounge. It is deserted for the moment, the smell of beer and cannabis from last night having not entirely dissipated.

'So, Mark,' I say, by way of ejecting him from his morning-after stupor, 'how did a fellow from Nippers Harbour end up doing grad work in Earth Science?'

He opens both eyes. 'The Lion we calls it. Ever been to Nippers Harbour?'

Can't say I have. But I did Google it last night. 'In Notre Dame Bay, right? Partway up the Baie Verte Peninsula.'

'Right on. Nippers Harbour got this humungous sea stack, shaped like a lion. All the time growing up, I was thinking, how the frig did that get there? Got interested in geology, you know, like you would.'

Sounds logical to me.

'So here I am. Researching coastal erosion. In my spare time building a database of sea stacks found along the coast of Newfoundland.'

'Useful undertaking no doubt.'

'You'd be surprised.'

Mark is part of the new generation of young outport Newfoundlanders. Steeped in the traditions and dialect of where he came from, yet self-confident, not the least bit intimidated by the big city boys, the "townies," who cross paths with him.

Having Mark alone presents opportunities. 'What was your take on Simón? A smart dude?'

'He was that, all right.'

'Anyone he didn't get along with?'

'Not for me to know. We were never like buddy-buddy. We didn't hang out all that much. But he was around. I'd tell him about Newfoundland, he'd tell me about Mexico. Last week he showed us all how to make tacos, real tacos, not the packaged shit you buy in the grocery stores.' Mark starts to choke up. 'Shit, man, I still can't believe it.'

Katerina appears at that moment, a trail of other students behind her, ones I haven't met yet. Jón is not to be seen.

As it turns out, about half of them are from Newfoundland, half from away. What they have in common is that they all knew Simón, to varying degrees.

When Jón does show up, subdued as expected, we have moved furniture to create something of a semi-circle. I invite him to have a seat.

He's uncomfortable from the start. It becomes obvious that he's the one everyone is expecting to take the lead in answering whatever questions I might have. I gather that, of all of them, he was the closest to the murder victim. The two were pals in the way that Simón and Mark weren't.

'Get your car back?' someone says to him.

He doesn't answer right away, then shakes his head slightly. I don't think much of it until another guy adds, 'I guess the cops impounded it for forensic examination.'

Jón doesn't have much choice but to provide an explanation. It comes out that he lent Simón his car to drive to Gros Morne. A Toyota which has seen better days apparently, but still works fine.

'What colour?'

'Red.'

I vaguely remember it parked at the foot of the Tablelands. 'It was getting late in the tourist season. Not many cars on the lot. Red comes to mind.'

If nothing else, it's a lead into the reason for this Sunday morning rendezvous. No need to repeat most of what I told the threesome yesterday, aside from the fact that I'm legit. They look skeptical, but that would be par for the course. Until such time as I can point to another case and name the bastard I put behind bars.

In the meantime I get right to the point. 'I want you to think very carefully. I want you to think back to the time you first met Simón. What struck you about him? What stood out? You knew him. I didn't. I want you to help me form a picture in my mind, as if I'm the one meeting him, right now, for the very first time.'

They hold back. A couple of them look toward Jón, who looks adamant he won't be the first to open his mouth.

'He spoke very good English. I knew he grew up in Mexico.

I was expecting an accent.'

'If he did have a slight accent, it was Texan.' A few others nod in agreement, with weak smiles. There's a longer pause.

'I mean, not to the point of being vain, but he liked clothes. He spent a lot of time on his hair. He was a bit of a metrosexual.'

That raises my eyebrows. Really?

I'm not exactly sure what that means. I have my theories.

'Let's face it,' pipes up a young woman who has said nothing up to now. 'Simón was fire.'

As in hot?

'He was a lad, all right.'

A lad?

'"Brohemian." He called himself a "brohemian."'

'For a laugh,' says Mark. 'He was havin' ya on. I called him *hombre*, in the ironical sense of course. He loved it.'

My head is swirling with synonyms. Millennial slang overkill.

I take a break by writing a few lines in the notebook. Followed by a deep, but inconspicuous, breath.

'Shall we move on then?' As if there's a choice in the matter. 'Good. I want to focus next on his area of research. Would someone fill me in? Why was he on the Tablelands that day?'

I'm prepared for something that will further challenge my knowledge of geology.

'He spent a week there in September,' says Mark, 'first when he arrived.' Mark looks at me and smiles. That's followed by the proverbial head nod and wink. 'Simón had a thing for ultramafic rock,' he quips.

Whatever ultramafic rock might be. If it's Mark's attempt to lighten the atmosphere, he's failed.

Jón's voice swells above the crowd. 'Simón was ultra-serious about his research. And if you want to know the truth, he was fucking brilliant!'

With the resounding expletive he has trenched a line in the sand. There is an audible rush to silence.

Jón recoils slightly, alert to the fact that he's made too much of a show of himself and his loyalty to his deceased friend.

Someone finally cracks the silence, 'Who's for a jolt of caffeine?'

Collective relief and approval. A couple of them make for the adjacent kitchen, and in due course mugs of coffee, like adult pacifiers, soothe the gathering.

'Is there anyone who can help me out on this one?' Here goes. 'Was there any indication he had enemies? Beyond mere jealousy.'

Long, contemplative sips of coffee.

'You mean enemy enough to do him in?'

'Not necessarily. At least for you to know. Even a small hint about a past relationship gone wrong. Problems at home in Mexico. Problems with the research he was doing.'

It draws successive blanks.

'Really? Nothing?'

Finally, Jón has an offering. A way to redeem himself perhaps. 'His father died years ago. He didn't get along with his stepfather, I know that.'

Not exactly an unfamiliar tale.

But I do feel a bit of leverage here. Enough to press him further. 'What else?'

He yields. 'His stepfather has money. Figured Simón should have been doing more with his life than going to university. Wanted to set him up in business. That's it. That's all I know.'

It's something. It's a start. Though I hardly think even a stepfather would be such a philistine he would resort to murder. Still, stranger things have happened.

We're not together much longer before some of them start

to drift away. Assignments due. Course readings to catch up on. Brunch reservations. In any case, I seem to have extracted all the information that could prove useful. Which doesn't seem like a lot.

I can't leave it at that. If there is still something to be uncovered, my bet is it will come from Simón's Icelandic pal. As he's about to leave and go back to his room, I draw him aside.

'Listen, no need to be embarrassed. He obviously meant a lot to you.'

He stares at me for a moment. There's a measure of disdain that he can't quite mask. 'I'm not the jealous lover, if that's what you're thinking. Not that anyone should give a shit about our relationship.'

I'm not quite quick enough in saying it. 'I certainly don't.'

'I doubt that. Am I your suspect number one? Did him in because he was two-timing me?'

If I'm being honest that was a theory. One of many. A PI covers all bases.

'I have a proposal.' One now with a different objective, if Jón is to be believed. 'I'm driving to Gros Morne in a few days. I need to check in with the cops out there. You're welcome to come along. I'm thinking you need to pick up your car.' No response. 'We could take a walk on the Tablelands. I could show you where it happened, if you want, if you think it might bring you some closure.'

Still nothing. I tear a piece of paper from the back of my notebook and scratch a number on it. 'This is my cell. Think about what I said. I can work around your schedule.'

He hesitates, but he does take the scrap of paper. He folds it and puts it in a back pocket, then walks off.

I'm thinking there's only a slight chance he'll want to go. But there's a chance.

The exit from the Signal Hill Campus is not uneventful. Just as I go out the front entrance an RCMP officer approaches. I hold the door open for her.

'Thank you.'

'No problem.'

She's all business. No need to wonder what that business might be.

It's mid-October. Colder weather has seeped into the city. I zipper up my jacket. Odd then to see someone striding across the parking lot dressed in a sports coat. The same one I'd seen him wearing in the summer, when our paths last crossed.

'Sebastian.'

His hand is cold even if he would have me believe the rest of him is not. Is he suggesting that all his toning in the gym provides a thermal shield?

'Frederick.'

He's wondering what I am doing here. I, on the other hand, I know exactly what he is doing here.

Nevertheless, it is only logical that I should ask. 'You're on the Simón Torres case? I believe the officer in charge just arrived.'

'You and Nick had a rough time of it.'

"Nick" is it now. Bit too chummy for my liking.

'We survived.'

'Sebastian, be careful where you go with this. It's a very active investigation.'

'I like to keep active. Out for a drive, you know, around town.'

'You're stepping into police territory.'

'I know my boundaries.'

'You're new at this game. Stick to the rules. Who hired you?'

'That, my friend, is confidential.'

'Perhaps I should reword the question. Did anyone hire you?'

'You mean am I getting involved merely out of the goodness of my heart?'

He half smiles, likely that half against his better judgment.

'Have it your way. Don't say I didn't warn you.'

'Cross my heart.'

'And?'

Now it is my turn to smile.

'Frederick, I have a question. Well, maybe two.'

'I have the right to remain silent.'

'The autopsy revealed nothing new. His throat was slashed after he was dead, correct?'

He hesitates.

'Nick and I figured as much. Otherwise there would have been more blood. What was the actual cause of death?'

'There'll be an official report.'

'I can't wait that long.'

He's not budging.

'I'll keep my distance. If I find out anything, the police will be the first to know.' Not a crack in the armour. 'Past experience, remember. Two heads on a case are better than one.'

Why he gives in, I'm not sure. I did almost get myself killed that first time around, before I had the training. He saved my ass in the end, but not before I had uncovered plenty to help solve the case for the cops.

'Strangulation.'

'You serious?'

Beyond that I'm struck dumb. Strangulation?

He jumps past it. 'What's your second question?'

'Has anyone shown up to claim the body?'

'His aunt arrives tomorrow.'

'I need to talk to her. What's her name? Where's she staying?'

'Your source has run dry. You're on your own.'

He moves past me, and through the second set of doors.
I call after him. 'Jón is from Iceland originally. Fine fellow. Give him my best.'

Strangulation? Maybe the murderer slit Simón's throat to disguise the fact he had strangled him. Didn't have much faith in forensics if he did. I need more time to think about this. I need to push the inspector for more detail.

Frederick is more decent than I give him credit for. He's taken over where I left off with my ex-wife, and having more success by the look of it. Nick is determined not to like him, which I understand, and from which, if I'm honest, I glean a measure of satisfaction.

Keeping an open mind (my inclination, most days) leads straight to the conclusion that I have to maintain a relationship with him if I'm to get anywhere with this investigation. That goes both ways. It's in his interest to keep on good terms with me, if he's ever going to be on good terms with my son. Do I have him over some type of barrel? Tempting though it is to think so, I wouldn't go that far.

I should invite Frederick to the house for a single malt. We need to get down to common denominators. I write it in my notebook.

There are plenty of other things occupying my mind for the moment. Simón's aunt for one, and how to make contact with her. As I drive back home, I see two possibilities. One is to contact the office of the Chief Medical Examiner; she will have connected with it to make the arrangements for the body. The other is to try to figure out the most likely flight for her to be taking, and see if I can spot her at the airport when she arrives. Neither are particularly promising.

Gaffer needs a walk, and since the son has yet to appear as scheduled to perform the duty, I am in the door and out again in the time it takes to get the dog snug in his harness. Gaffer dutifully follows my initiative. He's a smart mutt. Does what's expected of him, except for barking a blue streak when he encounters a dog he doesn't like, which happens to be most of them. He's a people dog. And on days when I'm a dog person, we are made for each other.

Nick still hasn't shown up by the time I return, which is a little odd, it being Sunday. I text him. *–What's up?* For which there is probably a slang version reduced to two characters that I don't know about.

When he does get back to me, fifteen minutes later, uncommonly long for him, it's a single emoji, a smiley with his hands upturned. Is it what I think it is—a shrug?

–Gaffer is dying to see you.

–okay

–when you coming over?

–soon

I leave it at that. Parents worry. Unnecessarily, most of the time. I have faith this is one of those times.

It's another hour before he turns up. Gaffer goes mad, even though it's only been a day since he's seen him. Nick tries to look interested. Something is not right.

'Sit down. Talk to me.'

He doesn't want to talk.

'Did you get a good night's sleep?'

'It was okay.'

'Just okay?'

He mumbles, 'Yeah.'

Something's worrying him. Do I need to steel myself for this one? The last time he confessed he was worried it was nothing a deodorant didn't cure.

'Out with it.'

He shakes his head.

'Nick, man, I'm your father. You can tell me.'
He shakes his head again.
'Is it personal?'
Still doesn't say anything.
'It is, isn't it?' Here goes. 'Is it something about your private parts?'
Eventually, 'Kind of.'
'Is something sore?'
He shakes his head.
'Erections are normal for a kid your age. When it's the last thing you want. Embarrassing, right?'
'I think I might be gay.'

Let's take a break, shall we? Let me wander into the kitchen and refresh my coffee. Let me allow myself some breathing space before reentering the room.
I sit on the couch next to him. 'Let me begin by saying I have no problem with you being gay should it turn out that way. One of my best friends is gay. Jeremy, right?'
'He's been gay forever.'
'Well, not exactly forever. He was married once, to a woman. It didn't work out.'
'See.'
'Nick, you're thirteen. Don't you think you're a bit young to come to this conclusion?'
'I don't have a girlfriend, do I? Lots of guys in my class have girlfriends.'
'Really? I didn't have a girlfriend until I was, I dunno, fifteen. Besides, that has nothing to do with it. Your hormones haven't really kicked in yet. When they do, watch out. I could tell you a few stories.'
'Dad, please.' He frowns, like I'm on another planet.
'I'm just trying to be realistic.'

'"Optimistic" you mean.'

So much for that approach.

'Are you attracted to other boys? Your best friend Tyler, are you attracted to him? Is that it?'

'Nooo. Besides, he's got a girlfriend.'

'Since when?'

'Since we were away, you and me.'

'Is she nice to you.'

'She's okay.'

I have a theory. I have to be careful.

'Is Tyler spending lots of time with her?'

'Of course. Wouldn't you, if you had a girlfriend?'

'Which means he doesn't have the time to spend with you. Maybe you're just jealous, that's all.'

'Jealous? Of Chloe? You got to be kidding.'

'Think about it. In a way, she's stolen your friend. I would be pissed off too, if I were you. You and Tyler were best buds. You did everything together. I bet he doesn't even text you, not like he used to.'

He won't admit it.

'Give yourself a break, pal. Maybe you will turn out to be gay. If so, I'm on your side. In the meantime, don't sweat it.'

He shrugs. I let him shrug. No comment.

'Are you sure you don't want to hear the story? Her name was…'

'Dad, pleeese.'

I shrug.

5

YOU WANT YOUR son to be happy. You want that above all else.

From the moment the kid is born, you wake up in the morning never quite knowing what the outside world is about to hurl his way. I like to think I've prepared Nick to hold his own, but there are a lot of pressures for a thirteen-year-old finding his way in the world. Figuring out who he is.

Let alone for someone who a week ago stumbled on a dead, mutilated body. That scene has got to be playing over and over in his head, got to be screwing around with his psyche.

All this is playing around in my own head as I sit within view of the escalator and adjacent stairwell, one of which every passenger deplaning at St. John's International must take to reach the baggage carousels. Except if the person has a mobility issue and needs to take the elevator, which I'm assuming doesn't apply to Simón's aunt. And except for those who have to clear customs, which also doesn't apply since she would have done that in Toronto, given the only connection between Mexico City and Newfoundland is through Toronto.

It's a smart-looking, relatively new airport. It handles about thirty incoming flights a day, so anyone waiting to meet a passenger gets to hang out near the escalator and stairs. In my case, trying to look like I know exactly who I'm waiting for, something which is becoming increasingly difficult to do. Two possible flights have landed, and I've had zero success. No Mexican-looking woman, in her forties at least, travelling alone.

I made two approaches on the off chance she wasn't Mexican by birth, that she had maybe crossed the border from the U.S., discovered it was a great country and ended up settling there. 'Excuse me, would you happen to be the aunt of Simón Torres? I'm involved in the case...' Each time I was met with stiff frowns before getting it all out. One woman accused me of the worse pick-up line ever. I smiled warmly and slipped back to the bench where I'd been sitting.

The security guard is starting to think I should have more to do with my time.

'You've been here for quite a while, sir. Is there something I can help you with?'

"Sir" is good. 'Not sure which flight,' I explain. 'We forgot to exchange cell numbers.'

I doubt if he's convinced, but he leaves me to fiddle with my phone, simulating busyness.

Given her possible connection times, my best bet is due at any minute.

For this one I am on my feet and at the ready. There is a steady stream of passengers looking relieved to be out of Toronto. To judge by the barrage of hugs and kisses, I suspect many of them are back where they were born and raised and have their swarms of relatives.

Not one looking the least bit Mexican, middle-aged, and alone.

I'm mistaken. No ifs-ands-or-buts mistaken.

She's decided to take the stairs, which sets her attributes in motion. She is carrying only a handbag over her shoulder, while most everyone else is loaded down with carry-on to save money. Her dark brown hair cascades over the shoulders of a tight-fitting salmon-coloured trench coat, that ends well above the knee and gives way to jean leggings and heels to match the coat. She's Latina through and through.

She could look forty-ish, but not because she wants to. She's the one, or my PI instincts have blown a fuse.

I constrain myself and wait until she has a few moments hanging loose near the baggage carousel before wandering in her direction.

'Excuse me.'

She turns and hits me with dark, troubled eyes.

'*Sí?*'

Utter confirmation, *sí*, that she's the one. But a potential problem. I took Introductory Spanish thirty years ago.

'*Mi nombre es* Sebastian Synard.' At least I remembered that much.

She smiles. It could be my butchering of her language. Or it could just be my name.

I blush, which is not difficult to do given the way her eyes have set my internal sensors bleeping.

'Yes, *Señor* Synard, what can I do it for you?'

Ah, but she does speak English, of a sort. Immense relief. I suspected as much, to be honest. A necessity for a woman who looks so worldly.

'I am a private investigator. I am working on the case of Simón Torres. Could it be that he was your nephew?'

Her hand springs to her mouth. '*Sí.*'

She wipes the corners of her eyes. I feel the urge to lay a comforting hand on her shoulder, but decide it is best if I restrain myself.

She recovers quickly. 'I am sorry, *señor*. I still cannot believe it.'

'I understand. It has been a total shock to all his friends here.'

'Who are you working for?'

The age-old question, one that apparently knows no border. 'No one but myself at the moment. You see, there is a personal reason I took on the case. My son and I were the ones who discovered the body, by accident of course.'

Her hand returns to her mouth.

Again I have to restrain myself. 'I'm so sorry.'

'Was it bad?'

The carousel is suddenly activated and the first bags appear through the chute. It's a blessing. This is not the place for such a conversation. Instead, I offer to collect her luggage.

She points to a modest-sized, but obviously expensive, bag when it loops around near us.

Delivered to her, handle extended, ready to be led away. 'May I offer you a ride to your hotel?'

She hesitates, then decides against it. 'I take a taxi. I do not know you, *señor*.'

That was what I was hoping to change. But, of course, the point remains unspoken.

'I understand. Would you instead consider meeting me tomorrow to discuss the case?'

'Perhaps. I am meeting the police. We have arrangements to make. I have time in the evening maybe.'

'Could we have dinner together?'

She will not commit. 'Call me at the hotel later in the afternoon. I see how I am feeling.'

We walk together to the exit, to a queue of taxis. 'Which hotel?'

'The Sheraton.'

A pity, given I live on Military Road and a stone's throw from the Sheraton.

'And who shall I ask for when I call?'

'What do you mean? You ask for me of course.'

Awkward. 'I'm afraid I don't know your name.'

Even more awkward when she opens her purse and removes a card, then places it in my hand.

The driver takes her bag and deposits it in the trunk. She steps ever so attractively into the taxi. I close the door. The taxi drives away.

Gabriela Ximena Estefania Ojeda.

Right. I'm suddenly feeling better about my own name.

Hers is beautifully inscribed on a drawing of a liquor bottle, as if it were the label. The promising, but sole words on the card. Gabriela is a name I can pronounce with confidence. As for the three that follow, there's plenty of incentive to learn.

My first foray into sleuthing taught me the value of search engines. When I return home I make for the leather La-Z-Boy, after a momentary side trip to the kitchen table for my laptop and to the beverage cabinet for the much-anticipated dram. That would be Laphroaig Quarter Cask. Gaffer loves the ritual—the tired master, a smoky dram, the comfy chair. He comes bounding up and onto my lap. He expects a behind-the-ears scratch before curling into the narrow space between my thigh and the arm of the chair. He prefers my lap, but is content to lie where he is, his head resting on the corner of the open computer just below the keyboard. My laptop lap dog.

Googling "Gabriela Ximena Estefania Ojeda" leads nowhere, but by eliminating one middle name and then the other, and searching through dozens of images, I eventually land in a place called San Miguel de Allende, which Google Maps tells me is a small city north of Mexico City. It's Gabriela all right, looking even more thought-provoking beside a pool than she does beside a baggage carousel. Salmon seems to be a favourite colour, though in this picture there is less of it covering her.

If that's her house in the background, it indicates money and a substantial amount of it. There's a tall vase of flowers and a cocktail on the table next to the patio chair. A margarita most likely. Hopefully not some high-end whisky gone to waste.

When I go past the picture and into the website, I find it's a posting to a holiday blog. At least that's what Google Translate leads me to believe. Someone from Barcelona writing a blog from the angle of a solo female traveller in Mexico. Gabriela (or Gabi as the day wore on and the margaritas continued) turns out to be a friend showing her the charms of San Miguel. Interesting. Seems they liked going to a club that features a male flamenco dancer.

My conclusions:

1) Gabi Ojeda has money and likes a good time.
2) She has a great deal of experience with tequila.
3) There is no significant other in the picture.

She doesn't have any Facebook presence that I can find. 'Maybe she uses a fake name,' my son yells out to me from the kitchen (head in the refrigerator by the sound of it). He's shown up after basketball practice, a pit stop before heading to his other place of residence.

He seems to have moved past the Tyler situation. I was going to ask when he came through the door and straight for Gaffer, but I thought, no, leave well enough alone.

I hesitated to tell him much about developments with the case, but I think it's only fair that I keep him somewhat in the loop. He planks himself on the couch with a bowlful of leftovers just out of the microwave. Gaffer immediately takes to the couch beside him, staring expectantly. The dog knows he's not to be fed except from his dish on the kitchen floor. He lives in hope, thinking if he waits long enough, Nick will cave and slip him something.

'Give Instagram a try.'

Instagram. Something else to waste my time. Not interested.

Five minutes later Nick has me set up. He's decided I should have it under my blog name as a way of "boosting its profile." A way to "up your hits," as he says. All sounds vaguely devious to me.

'Full name?' he asks.

Nick is on a search. I'm learning fast. I hand him the card.

He looks at me. 'Seriously?'

'Give it a go.' I spell the four names for him.

Nothing.

'This time we'll cut the Estefania.'

Nothing.

'Leave in the Estefania, cut the Ximena.'

Nothing.

We're down to Gabriela Ojeda.

Up pops an iPhone load of possibilities, each with a small circular photo. Rather provocative, some of them. What do these women get up to?

'I'm not sure you should be looking at this.'

He turns to me like I'm not from the known universe. 'Scroll down. See if there is anyone you recognize.'

Scroll. I might recognize the pose. Scroll. But not the individual. Scroll.

Nothing. No one.

Suddenly an inspired thought. 'Try Gabi Ojeda. Gabi— one "b", one "i", no "e".'

Nothing. Until, almost done scrolling... 'That's her,' I declare excitedly. 'I think.'

'Let's hope her account is not private.'

With a tap of the finger there she is indeed, gabiojeda27, the not-yet-bereaved aunt of the murdered Simón.

gabiojeda27 has an absorbing profile, once the translation activates. Her Instagram profile, not her actual profile, although that's rather absorbing as well, given the number of selfies she's posted over the past several months. I gather she works with a company that markets a range of high-end tequilas. Brands I don't recognize, given they're nothing like the *el cheapos* that clog the shelves of my local liquor outlet. In any case, my taste for drink has never yet leaned toward that potent Mexican option.

Not to say I couldn't be persuaded, depending on who might be salting the rim.

Gabriela's postings confirm the fact she knows her way around a margarita, though her outreach to potential clients involves an array of tequila cocktails, the names of which I have no clue.

Does she really like to drink that much, or is it merely in the line of duty?

I soon find out. The call to her hotel late the following afternoon yields agreement to get together for, not dinner as I had proposed, but 'a drink and something light.' 'It's been a long day,' she sighs.

"Light" could mean a lot of things, but I know the perfect, sophisticated spot, and it being a weekday, there's a good chance of a couple of seats at the bar. Or, with luck, a smallish table. I give Raymond's a quick call and the stars appear to be in alignment.

It's a two-minute walk from my house to the anticipated rendezvous at the Sheraton. Gabriela meets me in the lobby, emerging from the elevator in a thin, black V-neck sweater, skinny black jeans, and a colourful wraparound shawl that might have been flamboyant if she were to let it hang loose. She holds it against herself, in anticipation of the October weather she's experienced already today.

Raymond's is within short walking distance of the Sheraton. A cab is an option, of course, depending on how much of a toll her day has taken. Although the heels she's wearing could prove a problem on an incline, of which there are more than a few in downtown St. John's.

She's game, nonetheless. 'The sidewalks in San Miguel are jerky stone,' she informs me. 'Jerky stone sidewalks are hell on ankles.' *Jerky* stone. I try to decode it. In vain.

We're hardly out the front entrance door when the sidewalk takes a relatively gentle dip to Duckworth Street. I volunteer an arm. She chuckles.

Her independent spirit plants itself from the start. Remains there when the incline sharpens to Water Street. All the way to the steps leading up to Raymond's.

Raymond's is the premier restaurant in the city. If Michelin were ever to include Canada in its dispersal of stars, then I'd bet it would nab one or two. My wallet can't sustain the impact of the main dining room, but its adjacent bar I manage infrequently. Drinks, together with something surprising on a couple of small plates.

Gabriela is impressed, not least by the tequila cocktail. I'm impressed, not least by Gabriela's willingness to give herself over to the experience, all the while appearing undaunted by what she's had to deal with in the course of the day.

I don't question what exactly that turned out to be. I won't have her thinking I'm trying to pry into her family affairs. Still, she should know I have her best interests at heart.

'The other graduate students were devastated,' I tell her. 'Your nephew was very well liked.'

She looks me in the eye, the cocktail set aside. She says nothing. Her face slowly collapses into tears. Any attempt to control them falls away. She has laid her heart bare and my own heart laments for her.

I reach my hand across the table and rest it over hers.

She slips it away and brings both hands to her face, her perfectly manicured fingernails pressing against her mouth, her eyes closed.

When, finally, she has the wherewithal to speak, the words are surprisingly clear. 'Someone had to hate him to do this.'

'Hate. Perhaps. Jealousy. Perhaps. Revenge. Insanity. I have my theories.'

'Let's hear them,' she says.

I'm not that quick off the mark. 'Let's just say I need more time to investigate.'

'Who's paying you to do this?'

The relentless question. One I don't answer. My hesitation would appear to be answer enough.

'In that case, I will.'

I'm lost for words.

'God knows, I'm desperate,' she adds.

I prefer to think of "desperate" as in an urgent need for action. Bold and strong.

'I won't be in your Newfoundland much longer. I will take the urn and go.'

A rather sobering abruptness. 'I see.'

'As fast as all the papers are signed.'

I gather that cremation is the judicious option. The family in Mexico would take little comfort in a mutilated body arriving by Air Canada. Once the medical examiner and the police are finished with them, the remains will be turned over to a funeral home, as required by law, in order that preparations be made for cremation and the repatriation of the ashes to Mexico. Which all takes time. A lot of red tape, no doubt.

Gabriela is not a patient woman. 'I have to get back to work.

'And Simón's mother is desperate.'
  'Yes, no doubt. She must be in urgent need of answers, just like Gabriela. She must be bold and strong to face all the uncertainty about what happened to her son. But it will take time. It is murder after all, of a young man with such a bright future, a budding geologist on the verge of great discoveries. Academia now so much the poorer. The RCMP and their buddy, Inspector Olsen, will be determined to leave no stone unturned.
  I assume Gabriela has been thoroughly questioned in an attempt to determine whether there might be a Mexican connection to Simón's demise. Undoubtedly the thought of drug cartels has rushed into the naïve police investigators' minds, but that would be barking up the wrong tree. I've talked to enough of Simón's friends to put that one on the back burner. The fellow was far from a drug trafficker. Enough of clichés.
  I'm building a portrait of the deceased, and Gabriela is a key. A picture of his student life in Canada will sharpen in the days ahead, but I have this access to his life in Mexico for only a brief period. I have to make the most of it.
  'I have a few questions?' A gentle, open-ended query. Nothing too specific to begin.
  'You want to know my nephew, you ask your questions. That's what I'm paying you for.'
  Gabriela has a certain bluntness that I attribute to her limited use of English. A nuanced vocabulary is somewhat out of reach.
  'How would you describe him, your nephew?'
  'Describe him? Sweet. He was a sweet man.'
  Not exactly helpful. 'What else?'
  'Charming.'
  My look is meant to encourage her to try harder.
  'Cute.'

'Inquisitive? Adventuresome?'

Both words escape her. Tougher than I had hoped. I don't want to be putting words in her mouth. Definitely out of bounds, according to the handbook.

'Would you say he liked to take chances?'

'He was a go-getter, as you people say. He like to go and get it done.'

Ummm. 'Like what?'

'University. His mother never went to university. His cousins, they never went to university. I never went to university. Simón, he goes and gets university done.'

'He must have made his family very proud.'

She hesitates. 'His *padrastro* not so much.'

The infamous stepfather, I assume. 'But surely, after Simón did so well.'

'Rich men not read.'

A bit of a generalization, but I get the gist.

'Antonio told Simón he waste his time. Call him a *pinche fresa*.'

Doesn't sound too healthy. I'll have to Google that one.

'Simón tell him go fuck himself.'

Skip Google. 'That didn't go over too well I take it.'

'Make his mother cry. Make me cry. We all cry except Antonio Ramírez. He tell Simón to get the hell out of his house or he feed him to the dogs. Antonio own two big dogs. They are mad to bite.'

'He threatened to kill him?'

'Antonio is all mouth. He always talk like he ready to kill people he don't like. Maybe this time it's true.'

'Did Simón move out?'

'Next month he move to Texas. He start university.'

'And what happened between terms? Did he go back home to see his mother.'

'Of course. He always love his mother. He always hate Antonio. He stay away from him. After a while he stay in Texas. He work for professors. Simón is very smart.'
'And then he came to Newfoundland.'
'Strange place, Newfoundland. Do you ever get heat? Simón must freeze here.'
'It's not that bad. In summer.'
'When is summer?'
'July. August.'
'The other ten months you're cold.'
'We dress for it.'
'I like warm sun on bare skin.'
I can picture it . 'And tequila. You love a cold margarita on a hot day.'
'Of course. You don't like tequila?'
'I prefer whisky.'
'Whisky is for people who need to make heat to keep warm. Tequila is for people who hang loose in heat and stay cool.'

Sounds like an ad tag line to me. Normally, I would defend the honourable dram. I let it pass, to keep her in a good place.

She doesn't stay there for long. The sadness of her day turns all else irrelevant. She needs recovery time.

Back at the hotel we linger in the lobby, but not for long. Long enough for me to hand my client a business card with my contact information.

She alone takes the elevator to her room. I'm left with a wad of questions. Is she serious about hiring me? If so, under what terms? Financial and otherwise.

Back home, Gaffer curled next to me, my laptop tells me that Antonio Ramírez of San Miguel de Allende owns a large construction company and seems to have numerous projects and a work force of over a hundred. Thriving, by the look of it. From what I gather about a fifth of San Miguel's population is ex-pat, mostly from the U.S. and Canada. Some are permanent, some migratory—Canadians to escape their winter, Americans to escape their summer. San Miguel is in the Central Highlands and its climate is near perfect. The seemingly perfect place to retire and build an elaborate house you couldn't afford back home. And Antonio is just the man to do it for you.

Gaffer jumps to the floor and stares up at me. His tactful, low whine indicates his most cherished walk of the day is due him. He knows that by late evening a subtle approach works far better than an out-and-out yelp. He knows I'm a sucker for his stare.

Outside, along the downtown streets, it's still refreshingly crisp. As seasons go, fall is my favourite. Summer is maddeningly short, but come September and October, a dependable virility sets in, and when temperatures are already beginning to plummet in the rest of the country (Winnipeg, Saskatoon, *et cetera, et cetera*), I bask in a light-weight puffer jacket. Snow is usually a month, or even two, away. Green Christmases are not uncommon. St. John's might be the windiest and foggiest city in Canada, but by heck, it is also the most invigorating.

Gaffer senses my enthusiasm. He picks up the pace to something approaching a brisk ramble along Water Street. The street is a mix of shops and boutiques that have closed for the day, a few restaurants soon to do the same, and a scattering of pubs bleeding Irish music, their entrances flanked by smokers animated by their alcohol. One attempts to engage the dog, while completely ignoring me.

'Hey, Fluff, what's up?' And immediately starts petting him.

Despite the effete moniker, Gaffer sees no need to be anything but sociable. He licks the boozer's open hand, as if it were a substantial treat. God knows what germs he is ingesting. If there's a trait that Gaffer lacks, it's discretion. He is willing to pour his affection onto anything on two legs.

I tug his lead and his dogself out of range of the questionable appendage and continue along the street.

'See ya, Fluff,' the fellow calls. 'Have a good one.'

Right. Gaffer looks back and yelps as if the guy needs a thank-you. I pick up the pace and ruminate on what it would cost in dog trainer fees to break him of the habit, and conclude it's not going to happen. I have other financial priorities.

The Rose and Thistle is still on the go, and though the boost of the tourist season has waned, the mid-week die-hard locals are out and about. Not far away is the infamous George Street, with its intense proliferation of bars. The street never runs quiet. It could be minus ten and there would still be a gaggle of single women in thin cotton jackets, high heels, and upper-thigh-length skirts angling from bar to bar, about to topple over at the first gust of wind. You would think the meat market would have its downtime, but apparently that doesn't happen. Not that I know from personal experience. I have my limits.

Even gawking is out of bounds. My eyes straight ahead, Gaffer dutifully at my heels, we climb the steps past Trapper John's and land on Duckworth Street, out of harm's way. It will take us back to home territory.

Duckworth is a milder version of Water Street. It has its noteworthy restaurants and shops, and a quintessential pair of pubs for fish and chips—the Duke of Duckworth and the Ship. Personal favourites, though Gaffer and I can do no more than sniff the air as we pass them by.

I realize it goes against the principles of canine diet, but Gaffer is a keener for the odd chip, as he is for a corner of a sour cream glazed donut that's been known to come his way. The truth is his sensors for Tim Hortons donuts are extraordinary. As we approach the Canadian icon that stands at the intersection of Duckworth and Prescott, there's a significant injection of dog adrenalin. He trots taller, and with profound anticipation. No doubt he recalls the numerous times he's looked out patiently from the passenger seat window when my car has parked near this very establishment.

'Not tonight, pal.'

He has a variable understanding of the concept of "no," depending on the intensity of his craving. He plants himself near the front entrance and refuses to budge. I tug at his lead, but he has dug in all four paws. The cure for his obstinance is to smile at passersby, pick up his fifteen pounds, and continue on until we're out of olfactory range.

As I am about to move off, whining dog firmly under my right arm, the entrance door opens and out steps Gabriela Ximena Estefania Ojeda, neither word of which I manage to get past my lips. Slightly dumbstruck, the two of us.

She is followed by the RCMP officer from two days ago, now in street attire, whom I recognize, but who doesn't recognize me. And then by one Frederick Olsen. An evening full of surprises.

It is Olsen who speaks. "Good evening. Out with your dog I see.' His keen powers of observation have kicked in. 'Sebastian Synard. Inspector Ailsa Bowmore.'

I shake a no-nonsense hand.

'And let me introduce Gabriela Ojeda.'

Nice pronounciation. He doesn't get to bask in it. 'We've met.'

Yes, full of surprises. On both sides. If the inspectors were needing to interview Ms. Ojeda further, I would have assumed a police station to be the more suitable venue. Tim Hortons, as popular as it is among law enforcement officers, doesn't quite fit the bill for probing questions concerning a brutal murder.

Ms. Ojeda's English continues to fail her. Her hurry to get back to the hotel after I forked out substantial funds for cocktails and hors d'oeuvres at Raymond's has suddenly lost its authenticity. It is up to Olsen to explain away their meeting at the ubiquitous coffee shop, where the public's ears are deftly attuned to all conversation around them, no doubt especially that of sexy, foreign, English-challenged women. Disentangle yourself from that one, Inspectors.

'Gabriela has a fondness for the apple fritter,' Ailsa Bowmore chooses to inform me.

'My favourite—the apple fritter,' Gabriela says, with rather too much enthusiasm. 'I had one this morning,' she adds by way of explanation, 'at the hospital.'

I turn to Inspector Bowmore. 'In the vicinity of the morgue I assume.'

Gaffer starts to whine. I swear he knows the words "apple fritter." That particular donut is a favourite of his, second only to the sour cream glazed.

'An apple fritter. Really?' I try to keep my cynicism from overpowering the moment.

'Good to see you, Sebastian,' says Olsen, and turning to Ms. Ojeda, 'I know you're anxious to get back to your hotel.' No doubt.

I watch as they cross the street to whatever unmarked police vehicle taxpayers happen to be supplying these days. The car pulls onto Duckworth and there is no reason to think it will find its way to anywhere but the hotel. Unless, that is, she gets another craving for the apple fritter.

I give them the benefit of the doubt. The Mexican lady is stressed. Chilled and stressed, dealing with the horrific demise of, by all indications, a favourite nephew. She needs emotional support. She's urgently in need of answers. She's twisted in many directions at once.

Gaffer and I arrive home, the eventful walk complete. He wags his tail and stares in anticipation of a treat. The dog insists on a piece of dried liver treat upon completion of each and every walk. As he sees it, compensation for good behaviour, though it hardly applies in this case. Gaffer is not, however, great at understanding cause and effect. I give him the treat anyway.

For the master, a modest dram to ease his unwinding after an eventful evening. I check my email. Apparently it's not over yet.

Subject line: *I hate fritter*.

Sent a few minutes before. From her hotel room I assume. Gabriela is not subtle, at least in English.

Fritter is disgusting. In Mexico we love our churros. Dipped in chocolate. I needed to talk to police. They tell me to come to Tim Horton and talk. I ate fritter to be nice and get answers to my questions. Disgusting fritter!

I don't think apple fritters are all that bad. In fact the fritter rates very high when people vote on their favorite donut at Tim Hortons. Of course it is not really a donut. It doesn't have a hole. Still…

Here I am imagining a debate on the likability of apple fritters with a key person in an unsolved murder case! Where is my mind? Where is my professionalism?

I immediately reply to her email.

Good evening, Ms. Ojeda,

I hope you have recovered from your visit to Tim Hortons.

I was surprised to see you in the company of the police, but I understand your need to find out all you can before you return to Mexico.

Would you like to get together for a proper dinner tomorrow evening? We can discuss the terms of my contact.

Wishing you a goodnight,

Sebastian

I haven't finished the Lagavulin before another email pops up, this one with the subject line *Goodnight and Goodbye.*

Thankfully, what follows is not so ominous.

Sebastian dear,

(That's very much better, though I have to concede that maybe Google Translate is messing with her.)

No time for dinner. The police say the body of my nephew will be released tomorrow. Then cremation. Then I go home with the ashes. Mr. Olsen is helping me with the arrangements. Perhaps I leave for Toronto tomorrow night. Then for Mexico the next day.

Send me contract by email. Then I send money by PayPal.

Good for me. Good for you?

Goodnight Mr. Sebastian.

My reply, quiet in its disappointment, is brief and to the point.

Good for me. Goodnight, Gabriela.

I add *dear* at the end, but erase it.

6

IT IS GOOD to cut loose from the drama of St. John's and strike the open road. There's an audible sense of relief. 'Ahhhh, the TransCanada.' I glance across to the passenger seat but there is no response. I do realize it was a bit excessive. But I am a man made for open spaces, and this island of ours has no shortage of them. With just over half a million Newfoundlanders on a land mass the size of England, you don't have to go far before human habitation dwindles to zilch.

Driving from one end of the island to the other will boost a vehicle's odometer by 900 kilometres. I'm not going quite that far, but I've a good eight hours driving time ahead of me. No doubt, after a few hundred of them, the relief of going rustic will wear off, considering it's only been two weeks since I last did this drive.

I'm counting on one thing to keep highway narcosis at bay, and that's the person occupying the passenger seat. Jón. It hasn't been promising so far. He's barely spoken since I picked him up at 7 a.m. from the Signal Hill Campus. I attribute that to universal early morning student lethargy. It doesn't seem to be wearing off.

We need coffee. Eventually we hit the metropolis of Goobies Junction. I jokingly offer to take his picture in front of Morris the Moose, the enterprising statue near the highway restaurant. 'No moose in Iceland, right? Your folks would love a picture of you and Morris.'

'No mosquitoes either,' he retorts, dryly.

'Really? How forward-thinking is that. Was that an initiative of the tourist industry?'

My humour continues to escape him, not that I'm trying particularly hard. I mean I think it is fantastic that there's a whole country without a single mosquito. Who knew? What a boon to summer.

I treat him to coffee and a breakfast sandwich. It does the trick, turns the taciturn young Icelander into a sluggish conversationalist. The poor bugger was famished. I recall being a university student and feeling perpetually hungry. I insist on more coffee and a second breakfast sandwich.

'It's not easy, I know,' I tell him when we're back on the highway, just hitting the speed limit, the traffic good-naturedly light, the summer road construction season mercifully over.

'What?'

'Dealing with it all.'

'The aunt is a nutcase.'

Thankfully I have a solid grip on the wheel. 'Really?' Trying not to show the jolt resulting from the fact that Gabriela tracked him down, and from the way he spit out "nutcase."

'She came on to me.'

'You're kidding.'

'She's old enough to be my mother.'

True enough. Though hardly the motherly type. Still, I can't quite picture it.

'She thought she would get me to talk more. As if I were holding something back about Simón.'

He resisted the temptation. If it was a temptation. I'm having trouble being objective. What would be a temptation for me might not be for this guy. Testosterone is more variable than I take it to be.

'Hard to resist?' It's the best I can do.

'You sound jealous.'

Not where I want this to be going.

'Listen, Mr. Synard…'

The least we can do is try breaking the age barrier. 'Call me Sebastian.'

He calls me nothing. 'You don't get it,' he says. 'Older women don't do it for me. I've had girlfriends. I'm not hard up.'

Had, I think. *Hard up*, I think. 'Not in the least?' I say.

'You're showing your age.'

There are times in life when the world repositions and, apparently, you've slipped into the cracks. A whole shift in sexual politics seems to have passed me by. I would have thought I would be able to relate to this guy. On a male-to-male level.

'You need to update your perspective.'

Really, Jón?

Really, this young Nordic upstart has got me pegged as out-of-date and out-of-touch.

I'm slightly pissed. I try not to show it. If you've got a point to make, make it. Get it off your chest. Cough it up.

'Spit it out,' finally gets past my lips.

'As Simón used to say, you love and learn. If there's one thing he taught me it's to never go into a relationship thinking it will last. Maybe there'll be one that will, but in the meantime grab onto the moment, make the most of it.'

I give him time.

'Of course I loved the guy. Plenty of us did. He attracted people and he liked to experiment. It was an intense few weeks, but it wasn't going to last. He knew it and he taught me to understand it. We stayed friends.' His voice falters.

It all sounds rational. But what I know of love, it's not rational. Hearts break and jealousy takes over.

'You'd moved on already?'

'I needed time. Then this happened.'

I walk lightly here. Jón's pain is knotted inside him and needs release. It must have been a jolt to his headspace that he conceded this much. I'm positive he never intended to.

'I understand.'

'You don't fucking understand.'

Okay.

I turn on the radio. They're playing k.d. lang. *Constant Craving*. Good old CBC, always willing to reach out to its audience. And if I change stations it says more than if I don't. Hopefully the song wasn't a hit in Iceland.

'She nailed it,' Jón says. Open to interpretation, I'm sure.

There's a long stretch where we don't talk. I'm never entirely comfortable with silence between two people sitting a foot away from each other.

As bad luck has it, there's a news update. The Torres murder is the third story of the day, right behind the drop in oil prices and the rise in the cost of living. I live in a province of subtle ironies.

> *The remains of Simón Torres, found murdered in Gros Morne National Park, have been released to the victim's aunt, who arrived earlier in the week from her home in Mexico. CBC has confirmed that cremation has taken place. Mr. Torres's aunt will be returning to Mexico with the ashes. A spokesman for the RCMP says the full results of the autopsy will be made public within a few days. In the meantime, the investigation continues. No arrests have been made.*

'I don't get it,' he says. 'Why the rush? Now that he's cremated, there's no going back to reexamine the body.'

'The family wanted closure. The office of the Chief Medical Examiner has loads of pictures. There's plenty of tissue and fluid samples.'

He's not so sure. 'She's used to getting what she wants.'

I'm not about to resurrect discussion of Ms. Ojeda. Eventually his train of thought dissipates.

I consider stopping at Gander for lunch, but rather than reignite my sibling guilt, I press on for another hour to Grand Falls. Mary Brown's chicken and taters will taste the same no matter where we stop.

Newfoundlanders love their Mary Brown's. Our own version of KFC, only better. If calories are not your concern then go for it I say, and even if they are, we're all entitled to indulge once in a while. It's almost an act of patriotism.

Jón should have no concerns about calorie intake. He's one of those svelte types made famous by probiotic yogurt commercials. Nevertheless, he opts for the snack chicken wrap, no sauce. The Big Mary combo does me just fine. I do manage to get him to try a couple of my taters, which makes him a step closer to fitting into the local culture.

I still haven't figured out the guy. A few days ago I had him on a list of tentative suspects, but he's dropped off, and with a decisive ring of relief on my part. Too nice a guy. Which sounds altogether naïve on my part, but what I saw of the corpse and what I see of him just don't compute.

He could still prove useful, however, whether he realizes it or not. Keep him talking and who knows what unintended morsel of information might emerge. It's certainly not doing much for the case to have him sipping wordlessly on a cup of herbal tea.

I'm hoping being back on the highway is more conducive to conversation. There's a two-hour, generally drudging stretch from Grand Falls to where we turn off the TransCanada at Deer Lake. If there's going to be a break-out from his guarded responses, then my approach will have to take a decisive turn to something with a keener edge.

Questioning is a fine art in the game of private investigation. I think of it as developing into one of my stronger suits.

'There's something that's been on my mind.'

No response, of the verbal kind at least.

'You're telling me Simón made the most of every day, but he must also have been looking ahead. What did he see as his future?'

'The PhD obviously. He was riding a wave. His research was gathering more and more attention. He'd been published in a significant journal.'

As I knew already. 'Weren't other students jealous?'

'Jealous enough to kill him? Don't be crazy.'

'What about the profs? Were they jealous? Academics can be very territorial.'

He cast it off with a dismissive huff. 'To the point of killing someone? Who would do that except a lunatic? University profs are not lunatics. They wouldn't have a job if they were.'

Both points debatable to my mind. There are lots of crazies out there and I have no doubt some of them have contorted their way into professorships.

'Think about it. He was on the path to becoming a world class geologist. Where he did his degrees would be a great endorsement for any university. The prof from the University of Texas couldn't sing his praises loud enough.' Jón takes a deep breath. 'You heard that.'

I admit I was impressed. 'I hadn't realized Simón was quite so highly regarded. I'll do a little research. See what I can find out about the professor. Make sure it was something he truly believed. Make sure he's legit.'

It wasn't the thing to say. Stifled silence from Jón, with slow burning scorn. 'Are you paid to be so damn skeptical, or does it come naturally?'

Touched a nerve. I let him vent, before bringing him back to reality. 'A PI looks at all the angles. Murder does nobody any favours.'

That last phrase is my own invention. I jotted it down in the margins of my course outline. It sat very well with me. Every PI needs a maxim, especially a PI with a reputation in need of a foundation.

'What do you know about Troy Foster? How is he regarded within the academic community?'

'Are you serious? His work on Gulf Basin Depositional Synthesis was groundbreaking. He's a major figure in his field.'

I can be forgiven. Not everyone is a geology nerd. "What did Simón say about him?'

I expect a stellar endorsement. What I get is hesitation. 'He didn't say much.' Jón quickly adds, 'Why should he? I didn't ask.'

I leave it at that. I can't let our relationship deteriorate. Jón is a key figure and, to be honest, I like the guy. He has a lot yet to experience about the ways of the world. But plenty of time in which to do it.

A bit of age envy at play on my part no doubt. Thinking back thirty years and who doesn't wonder at the life choices he's made. How different things might have been had I taken a different career path.

'Are you married?'

That too.

'Not anymore.'

He figures he shouldn't go any further.

'I have a son.' He knows that. He knows Nick's the one who discovered the body. 'I'd like you to meet him. He's a great kid.'

Not sure I should add this. 'He's a little confused about life at the moment. He could use a different perspective than mine.' I'm nothing if not foolhardy.

There's no need for him to think he needs to answer.

I turn up the radio. CBC Two is better at injecting something worthwhile into dead air.

I check the temptation to bear down on the accelerator a bit more. As it is I almost miss my favourite highway sign in the province—No Name Brook. I point to it frantically for the few seconds before we zip past.

'Must have been an off-day for cartographers.'

Not so much as a chuckle. It would seem my sense of humour is not dark enough for the Nordic soul.

While I'm at it I point out the sign for the access road leading to the community of Howley. 'Named after a famous Newfoundland geologist and explorer. And cartographer.'

'James P.'

'Absolutely. Don't know what the P stands for.'

'Pre-occupied.'

Ah, his wit finally making an appearance. And not particularly dark. All is good.

The turnoff from the TransCanada is a further half hour and at this point there's a noticeable change in the atmosphere. I turn on to Route 230, heading toward Bonne Bay.

I attribute the mood swing to the proximity of the Tablelands. Jón has never been there and the anticipation of confronting such a geological powerhouse is having a visceral impact, compounded of course by the fact that it's the site of his friend's demise.

I do my best to steady the yin yang at work in him. 'One step at a time. Let's stick together. Anytime you feel yourself agitated, we'll work it through.'

He takes a deep breath, which could mean a couple of

things. I veer in favour of a reflex to help steel himself for what lies ahead.

It is mid-afternoon by the time Jón gets his first view of the Tablelands. The fall sun is sinking low in the sky, intensifying the yellow-orange of the rockscape to something alien, otherworldly. These vast plant-toxic mounds leave him struggling for words.

I recall my own reaction when I first saw them. I can only imagine the gut reflex of a budding geologist.

He exits the car and wanders off, anxious it seems, for some alone time. As you would expect. Life has its pivotal moments that remain deeply private. I wander some distance behind on the path, as he veers off and finds a place to sit and ponder what surrounds him. I cautiously keep him within my line of vision.

The cell reception proves reasonable, and I luck into a message from Nick. He persuaded his mother to let Gaffer stay with them for the two days I'm away. He's eager to report that all is going great. At least from his perspective. I doubt it is from Samantha's. It'll do her good to see first-hand that Nick has another source of affection in his life.

Jón has had his moment. He wanders back in my direction. He is as prepared as he's ever going to be for what must follow.

I retrace the route Nick and I took on our ascent of the Tablelands. Jón is an adept hiker, but I insist we take our time. There's more than my own surefootedness to consider. Jón needs time to acclimatize, to deal mentally with the variations in the landscape. A sprained ankle at this point would not be good.

'Amazing,' he says, no doubt referring to the fact we're trekking the earth's mantle. 'The years add up.'

'Five hundred million of them.'

Now he chuckles.

What's that all about? Iceland has its own astounding geological features. Does he find them amusing as well?

We're not in the same headspace, but I let that pass. We will be, soon enough.

The shallow pool where Nick and I went for a dip doesn't look like it's changed any, though it's no doubt even chillier. Unlike the day of the previous encounter it is partially overcast, the water less inviting. Jón insists on removing his hiking boots and socks, and tugging up his pant legs (though not very far considering how tight they are). He steps into the water and finds a decently smooth place to stand. For what reason I'm not sure. Perhaps to recreate the actual experience from my perspective.

He doesn't wince at the cold. Then again I'd say the average healthy Icelander is not adverse to a plunge in ice-filled water before scampering back to a geothermal pool. I've seen pictures.

'Then I hear Nick yelling, terror in his voice.'

'Where was it coming from?'

I point to the general area.

He scrambles back into his hiking boots, just as I did. I lead the way. No need to run, though Jón is prepared to.

There's no sign of the police investigation, unless the viewer happens to have been there when it all happened. The rocks that partially covered the body have been returned to their original location, but only roughly to the same configuration, given the vacant space that was created by the removal of the body. They've also been turned bottom up so that the numbers they bear are no longer visible. A reasonably successful attempt at making it look like nothing has happened here. Parks Canada wouldn't want to see it turn into a shrine for a murder victim.

Yet, for the two of us that's what it is, for the time we are there. I don't encourage any questions, but Jón is anxious for details of how it looked on that fateful day.

A delicate task. Nothing to cause undue stress. Something to help him through the ordeal of seeing where his friend died.

'Simón was at peace. He might not have looked it at first…'
'Don't talk bullshit, Sebastian.'
A miscalculation.
'The rumour is his throat was slashed.'
A brief hesitation. 'Correct.'
'Give it to me straight.'
I do, in all its horrific detail, the strangulation and all, the so-called bullshit firmly set aside. I let the petulant young man deal with it.

By the time I'm through, he's in tears.

Of course I feel sorry for him. Nevertheless, if he's going to come to terms with it, now is the time to start. I move aside and let him have his time alone with the deathly expanse of rock.

Eventually he joins me for the walk back. In silence, until we have almost reached the base of the mountain.

'It seems the least likely place to commit a murder,' he says. 'Whoever did it must have known he was here. It wasn't random. He was targeted. Either that or they met up here and were hiking together.'

'Rule that out. Too much of a chance they would encounter other hikers. Someone who would see them together and remember what the other person looked like. The cops will have investigated that angle.'

'So someone was stalking him until Simón made the move to climb the mountain.'

'Could have been a hired killer. That way whoever wanted him dead wouldn't have to come near this place.'

'Regardless, he'd have to have some way of knowing Simón was headed here.'

Suddenly it dawns on Jón why he would be a suspect…or an accessory.

'There were lots more of us who knew.'

'I'm looking for someone who would have known, plus had

a reason to do him in.'
'Not just his university friends?'
'Anybody.'
'Male or female?'
I won't admit it, but I'd been thinking male, at least the person who pulled the knife across Simón's throat. 'Could be female.'
'But not likely.'
'Not *as* likely.' Can't figure I'm being sexist when I say that.
'Gay or straight?'
'No distinction.'
'Really?'
'Murder does nobody any favours.'
'You're sounding wise beyond your experience, Mr. Synard. Didn't you tell us this is your first real case.'
'Sebastian.'
There's a half-smile, a half-hearted one. 'Sebastian.'

The sun has set by the time we reach the parking lot. It would be another hour to the cop station in Rocky Harbour, so we decide to leave the retrieval of Jón's car until the morning. I booked us into a B&B in Woody Point and we'll show up there after finding a bite to eat.

The Old Loft is closed for the season, so a redo on the partridgeberry pie is off the list. What is still open is the Seaside Restaurant in Trout River, specializing in seafood, and I'm guessing there's never been an Icelander who didn't like seafood.

And, by God, we lap in together—mussels, followed by scallops, followed by pan-fried cod. Topped off with the much-prized bakeapple cheesecake. I find gluttony can sometimes do the trick, where conversation fails.

'You probably know them by a different name—cloud-berries. We call them bakeapples. Why? Because they taste a bit

like baked apple? Who knows?'
'We have them sprinkled on skyr.'
'Really. Skyr? Spell it.'
He adds, 'In the yoghurt section. Not as good as at home.'
It unearths a memory. 'My mother loved to pick berries.'
'As did mine.'
I think I might have seen it in the supermarket. I admit I'm not a fan of yogurt. When I do buy it, it lingers regretfully in the fridge well past its best-before date.
'Try skyr. You might like it.'
'Skyr.'
Fascinating how an innocent four-letter word can help solidify a relationship. I'm more convinced than ever that Jón had nothing to do with the murder. Bakeapples/murder/skyr—they don't add up. My gut instinct says no. Savage son-of-a-berrypicker—doesn't cut ice.

We check into Aunt Jane's Place, built over a hundred years ago and as the bronze plaque next to the front door notes, for many of those years "It was used as a tourist/boarding house and Sample Room by agents from schooners sailing the coast to display goods to merchants." The travelling salesmen stories these rooms could tell.

Tame in comparison to those who have gone before, we take to our respective rooms. We both have e-mails to catch up on, and Jón has a mid-term to study for. Yawn.

Within a half hour I'm rapping on his room door.

A muttering response, not quite English. Sounding like I woke him up, confirmed once the door opens.

'*Já.*'

'How about we grab a beer?'

'*Ókei.*'

He's back on linguistic track once we're in the fresh air.

'A craft beer,' he says. It seems that since he's been in

Newfoundland Jón has developed a fondness for the products of our microbreweries. He names a half dozen he's tried. By which time we have reached Galliott Studios, since nothing is far from anywhere in Woody Point. If there's a place in town where he'll find something new to him, this is likely it.

Nick and I had been here for breakfast on the fateful day. Galliott Studios sells coffee, light meals, art, and beer, in that order. The owner is a young entrepreneur determined to stay in rural Newfoundland when so many of her generation have up and left.

'A craft brew with a view,' I tell her. 'That's what we're looking for.'

'Yes!' says Jón, more alive than he's been all day, spying the logo of the Western Brewing Company.

It is late in the season for the deck experience, especially after dark, but leaning against the railing, a Wild Cove Pub Ale in hand, the scattered lights of Bonne Bay before us, there's no resisting the experience. Life with a beer doesn't get this good very often.

The owner seems to remember me. The chatter between us on my previous visit probably led to mentioning that Nick and I were off to climb the Tablelands. As details of the murder came out, she concluded we were the ones who found the body.

'How's your son doing?'

'He's good.'

She is genuinely concerned, but respects my privacy. The murder had to have hit Woody Point like a bombshell.

'No arrests?' Ask a question you already know the answer to, you never know where it might lead.

'Nothing that I've heard.'

'No reports of anyone suspicious around before it happened?'

She shakes her head. 'I'm thinking whoever did it wasn't

about to make himself known, before or after. He's long gone.'

She's jumped to the same gender-based conclusion I did, open-mindedness notwithstanding.

'The RCMP did find a ball cap apparently.'

'Really? That's it—a ball cap?'

'That's what I've heard.'

'Anything written on it?'

'That I don't know.'

Of course the cap could belong to anyone, not necessarily the murderer. Likely some careless hiker caught by a gust of wind. Likely a cap weathered and worn from months lying about the rocks.

Nevertheless, worth poking around, seeing if it might fit a killer.

Which is exactly what I attempt to do when Jón and I arrive at the RCMP station in Rocky Harbour early the following morning.

Staff Sergeant MacAvery is surprised, and no doubt inwardly disappointed, to see me. His attempt to cover the latter response with semi-cheerful chatter is only mildly successful. 'Mr Synard, you've returned.'

Jón had phoned him a couple of days ago to let him know he was coming to claim his vehicle. He hadn't mentioned how he planned to get here.

At that moment Constable Trottier appears from a back room. She, too, is surprised, but I'm unable to ascertain her level of disappointment. She smiles thinly. 'Mr. Synard.'

I take it as an opening to the questions I have listed in my mental notepad.

While the paperwork for the release of the vehicle is being prepared, I ease into the list. 'Anything new uncovered in the investigation that I should know about?'

'Our last public statement was two days ago. You would have heard it.'

I am not so easily dismissed. The staff sergeant's attempt to relegate me to the general bin of Joe Public requires a keen counter strategy. One for which I'm prepared. 'Don't you think it would be wise to let me see the cap considering it might trigger a memory of who had been wearing it? Nick and I passed a number of hikers sporting ball caps that morning.' (The number being maybe one or two.)

'What cap?'

I smile. I feel my eyebrows ascending. 'It's common knowledge in Woody Point.'

He hesitates, trying to look as if he has a choice in the matter. Surely he is not about to put the investigation before his ego. He exits to his office. I offer Constable Trottier a good-natured, nicely understated smirk.

The staff sergeant returns with a file folder. He opens it to reveal three colour 8x10s. He lays them down on the counter one at a time, forming a row directly in front of me. It would seem Constable Trottier's confidence with the camera has grown.

It's not your average ball cap. Rather smart-looking. And almost pristine, as if it had only been worn once or twice. Camouflage print, but upscale camouflage print. A dusty purple and olive. And dull silver patches. Definitely not your moose hunter type.

There's something stitched on it—a single line, across the front, just above the brim. Subtle, not meant to stand out. I hold up one of the photos for a closer look.

Reunite Pangaea. Get my Drift?

What the hell is that supposed to mean? I look up at MacAvery. Then pass the photograph to Jón, who has been peering over my shoulder.

'Recognize the cap?' MacAvery asks pointedly.

Not me. 'Afraid not, Staff Sergeant.'

'Didn't think so.' He plucks the photo from Jón's hand, shuffles all three back into the folder, and closes it firmly.

'Anything else I should know about? Any other way I might be useful to the investigation?'

'That's quite all right, Mr. Synard. Should your input be required I'll have Constable Trottier contact you.'

I look over at the constable who looks surprised to hear her name. I raise a consenting hand and give her the Newfoundland nod. She is unresponsive.

'Have a safe trip. Watch out for moose,' announces MacAvery. He places the keys to Jón's Toyota within his reach.

Our welcome has expired. The pseudo-efficient staff of the Rocky Harbour RCMP keenly await our exit.

It would be unreasonable of me not to offer a few parting words. 'I should tell you, Staff Sergeant, that my personal investigation is well underway, fully funded by the victim's aunt. I have unlimited resources to find the murderer. If I can be of any assistance to the RCMP, please contact my secretary. I'll likely see you at the trial, if not before. Have a great day.'

My back is turned and I am out the door without giving him a chance to counterattack. Jón closes the door behind us.

Jón is laughing. I have gained satisfaction on both sides of the door. I give the fellow a friendly pat on the back.

As we make a move to our respective vehicles, I'm thinking, rather than drive all that way into St. John's without seeing each other, maybe we could coordinate a few choice stops. I make an offer he won't refuse. 'How about we add to your compendium of Newfoundland microbreweries?'

He's game, absolutely. The lad likes his beer.

'First stop—Cormack. Crooked Feeder Brewing. It's a few kilometres off the highway, just before we get to Deer Lake. I'll go ahead. You follow me.'

'By the way,' he says. 'That cap belonged to Simón.'

That stops me in my tracks to the car. 'Really? Are you sure?'

He is. It's an hour later, after a chat with the super-friendly woman tending bar at the Crooked Feeder brewery, and the purchase of a couple of growlers of their finest to take back to St. John's. The Double Chocolate Oatmeal Stout is on tap and sounds like a good snack, but maybe not in the morning and at 7.1% abv.

A more driver-friendly Bakeapple Kombucha is also on the go. (A versatile berry, that bakeapple.) A half-pint of that, together with a cinnamon bun, which, as proudly noted, has been homebaked that very morning.

Between his first and second cinnamon buns, Jón tells me, 'He ordered the cap online, then had the words added.'

'And you opted not to enlighten those eager and efficient RCMP officers? But I don't get it—the words. I looked it up on my phone. Reunite Pangaea was the name of a band, now defunct. They played (quote, unquote) math rock. What the hell is math rock?'

'Google ripped you off.'

'Fire away.'

'Three hundred million years ago there was a single supercontinent—Pangaea. Before it broke up and started drifting apart to form the continents as we know them today.'

A light flickers. 'Geology humour.'

'Rid the world of racism. Let's come together as one. Simón was all about equality.'

'I thought he was all about geology?'

'Get my (quote, unquote) drift?'

The light is full on. 'Continental drift.'

He grins with a certain geological smugness. 'It was going to be the title of his upcoming paper in *Geology Today*.'

Reunite Pangaea. Get my Drift? It all sounds too subtle, too hip. Can geology really be hip? I thought it was all about traipsing through mosquito-plagued wilderness with a rock-pick hammer.

'Simón was a dude.'

Apparently so.

'Attracted more dudes to consider earth sciences as a career option.'

'Maybe including some weirdo willing to kill him. Maybe for a price.'

'I'm not sure you're making sense.'

I'm not sure either.

We exit this brewery for another, six hours later. We are forced to weigh our craft beer options. There's Split Rock in Twillingate, but it would require an hour detour off the TransCanada. Instead, we arrive in the town of Dildo, and seat ourselves in the restaurant of the Dildo Brewing Company.

True, it also requires a detour, but only a slight one. Driving into Dildo there's a couple taking a selfie in front of the "Welcome to Dildo" sign, a common sight. Dildo was made famous by ABC talk show host Jimmy Kimmel, who seemed to think repeated use of the name Dildo would boost his ratings. I have no idea if it did or not, but it definitely boosted tourism to Dildo. The town was besieged with tourists all summer and Dildo Brewing is laughing all the way to the bank.

'Make mine a pint of Stout Dildo.'

'Same for me. Stout Dildó.'

Gotta love the accent. So artificial penis is roughly the same in Icelandic as in English.

Jón is not sure what all the fuss is about. 'In Reykjavik we have a museum devoted to penises.'

Yes. A fact that, given my limited knowledge of Nordic cultural activity, I had not known. 'Built to shore up the economy?'

'The Icelandic Phallological Museum. Specimens from over 200 mammals. All preserved in individual jars. Or tanks, in the case of whales.'

Now there's a tidy bit of info to go with our platter of mozza sticks, cod bites, and pickle spears. 'Makes Dildo sound inconsequential,' I suggest.

'We all have our hang-ups.'

I'm not sure where he might go from here. Silence on my part could be the most judicious option. A swallow of stout, a bite of cod, a crunch of pickle, another swallow of stout.

'Even Simón.'

A swallow of stout, a stick of mozza, another swallow of stout.

'He had this fetish about cleanliness. He showered three, four times a day.'

'Seriously?'

'I know. Odd for a geologist.'

'What did he do when he was out in the field? All that hiking about, bound to get dirty and sweaty.'

'That's why he loved the Tablelands. Open space, no vegetation, no need to rough it in a tent. If he was hiking for a long time, he'd always keep an eye out for water, a pond or a lake.'

'A brook? You think maybe he went for a dip in that brook Nick and I went in, near where we found the body?'

'I'm sure of it.'

'But it was cold as hell.'

'Simón would have hated it, but he would have done it anyway. Once he arrived in Canada, he practiced. Started taking cold showers, so if he ever needed to take a dip in the wild, it wouldn't be so bad.'

I look at Jón. I don't buy it. Sounds like bullshit to me.

'When you went in that pool, did you notice any soap

bubbles? He used this product called Jack Black Turbo Wash. He ordered it online. Super expensive. I tried it once.'

'Sure you did. I chuckle, my skepticism not easily disguised. 'Do you remember the smell of juniper? That's the scent. It's very nice.'

I don't have it in me to say he's lying. Because, bloody yes, now I do remember. While I was standing there, knee deep in the water, freezing my ass off, I remember thinking if nothing else this smells like the great outdoors, except there's no outdoors around me except rock, no vegetation, no juniper that's for sure. Then Nick's yell drove it all out of my mind.

I admit it all. 'I don't recall smelling it off the dead body.' Which is a rather lame attempt at saving some face.

He huffs in my direction. He adds, 'So whoever strangled him did it when he was in the brook washing up.'

'Not so sure about that. That would mean the body would have had to be dragged or carried to the spot where he was found.'

'Were there any cuts or scrapes on his legs or feet? There would be if he were dragged over those rocks. Even if he were alive and forced at knife point to the spot, there would have to be some marks left on the soles of his feet. Unless he put his hiking boots back on. Which is highly unlikely.'

'No marks that I saw when we uncovered him, except for the indentations from the weight of the rocks.'

'Then most likely he was killed in the brook, then lifted up and carried.'

'He was pretty slim. I'd say no more than 150 pounds.' I resist the temptation to add "soaking wet."

'Would have taken a strong person.'

'Or two.'

Something else to put me off my game. 'Don't think so. Gets too complicated. Twice as much to go wrong.'

'Maybe. Maybe not.'

Jón is forcing my head in too many directions. I must maintain control. It's time to consolidate and theorize. 'Simón arrives at the Tablelands early in the morning, parks your car, sets off up the mountain. The killer shows up, keeps an eye on him in the distance, pretends he's out for a hike while Simón does his geology business. Idling, waiting for his chance. Once Simón decides to wash up in the brook, the guy pounces. Before Simón has a chance to react he grabs him by the throat. Carries the dead body to the spot, slits the throat to disguise the strangulation, then starts to cover him with rocks. Before he finishes the job he panics, races back to the brook, grabs all Simón's stuff, except for the hat which blew away, then gets the hell out, by a route no hikers are likely to take. Nick and I show up ten minutes later.'

'Plausible. Up to a point.'

What is this? Jón—suddenly having PI tendencies? He'll learn the hard way that you don't lay claim to it without preparation.

'What point?'

'The point at which the guy pounces,' Jón says. 'How could Simón not see him coming? The brook is out in the open. Simón was naked, soaping up, sure to be keeping an eye around him. He was not an exhibitionist, he just had this thing about being clean.'

'He was freezing cold. He got careless.'

'Doubtful. His stepfather was a tough bastard who was in with some shady characters and who hated him. He didn't get careless; careless wasn't in his nature.'

'Is that a theory? You've consolidated all you know, and this is what you've come up with? That Simon's death was a hit job orchestrated by his stepfather? Where's your evidence? A hunch is not enough.'

I take a deep breath to alleviate my irritation. The guy is jumping to conclusions without anything substantial to back them up, something we avoid in this business. I shouldn't be irritated. I should be understanding of his naiveté. I need to maintain a positive relationship. Another, deeper breath. A last swallow of Stout Dildo.

'His stepfather was pissed off with him.'

'We know that. Is he so ruthless he would arrange for the murder of his own stepson, his wife's only child?'

'Maybe.'

'That's a pretty implausible *maybe*.'

'His aunt didn't rule it out.'

I could do with another swallow of Stout Dildo. 'She said that?'

'She volunteered the opinion.'

Okay. Set me back a notch or two. If what he says is true, when Gabriela Ximena Estefania Ojeda was in St. John's she was just as forthcoming with Jón as she had been with me, the hired man.

Now I get it. A calculated step toward putting the makes on him. The old bedroom tactic. Tell the potential sex partner something that sounds like an intimate, closely guarded secret and suddenly he/she feels special and is willing to dispense with a few items of clothing. Hop into bed and reveal his own secrets.

'Oldest trick in the book.' I serve him up the explanation, as discreetly as I can, not being versed in Nordic sexual practice.

Jón takes it as an affront to his good sense. His immaturity makes a sudden show of itself. 'Sounds like you've had first-hand experience. Did she play along?'

His pettiness not far behind. This is leading nowhere productive.

'Let's leave it at that, shall we? We need to be getting on the road.'

I get the waiter's attention. 'Two separate bills, please.'

I extend a hand in the parking lot and Jón shakes it with a certain rigidity.

It goes without saying I'll want to see him again. Despite the volatility of his common sense, he's still key to the investigation.

'*Bless*,' he says.

Odd, but I'll take it as an improvement. 'Bless you, too.'

'It's "goodbye" in Icelandic.'

7

IT'S SEVEN O'CLOCK and dark. I still have an hour to go before reaching St. John's. It's been a long haul. Darkness and fatigue boost the probability of a calamitous encounter with a moose. I think about Jón. He's heard my riff on how all 1200 pounds of a bull moose can spring onto the road from nowhere. At least Jón's not a yahoo speed demon; not with that aging Toyota, he's not.

Morris the Moose, caught in my high beams, reaffirms the odds. I turn off the highway and into the parking lot. Under such circumstances I have my coping strategy. Stop, take a fifteen-minute nap, then dig through the glove compartment for one of those unhealthful energy shots that I have stowed away for when I could use a quick boost of caffeine.

Just as I'm about to take to the highway again, there's a text from Nick.

–*Home soon? Need to talk.*
–*Back in an hour.* Plus smiley.

It's plenty to keep me awake.

All I want is to wind down with a sizable dram. Nick has other plans. He's at the house when I get there, he and Gaffer. To judge by the pile of dishes in the kitchen sink, the boy and dog returned to my place several hours ago. I await the confession.

'I didn't feel like going to school.'

'Were you sick?'

He shakes his head. At least he doesn't lie.

'Your mother know about this?'

'She was at work. I texted her when I figured she was back home.'

'So she doesn't know the whole story?'

'Could be.'

I have all the time in the world to get it out of him.

'How about I move in with you for a while?'

We've been through this before, too many times. Every second weekend. That's it. 'You know the custody...'

'It sucks.'

'It sucks for me, too.'

He grabs onto it. 'Change it then.'

'Your mother'd have a flying fit if I even suggested it.'

Not good. Not the thing to say.

'She's screwing things up for both of us.'

I pull him close, hug him into me. Last year was a bit rough, but I figured he'd gotten past it.

'I liked it better when you broke your hip.'

That's comforting.

'At least I got to spend more time with you.'

He was a great help when I was laid up, recovering. 'Perhaps I should consider falling over a cliff a second time.'

He's not smiling.

'Your mother loves you. You know that. You're number one in her life.'

'I doubt it.'

'Don't doubt it for a second.'

'What about asshole?'

I ignore the word, as much as I hate that it slipped out of his mouth so easily. He means Olsen of course. It's not beyond the realm of possibility that I've used the same descriptor in front of him, in reference to the same Inspector Olsen. Like father, like son. What goes around, comes around. I fail to come up with a third comforting truism.

'I thought you two were getting along. Personally, I like him better than I did before.'

'He wants to be buddy-buddy. It's not going to work.'

'Maybe he deserves points for trying.' I forced it out, even though the thought of Olsen playing dad-replacement galls me no end.

'Not from me.'

Chip off the old block. There's the third one.

Okay. We both need to face up to the fact that Olsen is not going to disappear from Nick's life anytime soon. He's planted himself firmly in Samantha's abode, and as far as I can tell, he intends to remain there.

'You need to get over it. The guy does have his good points.'

'Name one.'

'Nick, man, you can't see the forest for the trees.'

He glowers at me, his lip turned up. 'Speak English.'

'Your Mom likes him; he likes her. She needs him in her life.'

'She never asked for my opinion. It's my house, too.'

'She's in love with him, I guess.'

Actually I don't guess.

Nick looks at me intently, a storm brewing in his eyes.

I try again. 'You need to get over it.'

'He still sucks. The asshole.'

Gaffer saves me from myself. He's a perceptive mutt, that Gaffer. His timing is impeccable.

He wants attention. He sits and glares at us and starts to whine. Can't you two get along? What about me?

I rub his head affectionately. He jumps up on the couch between us, then onto Nick's lap.

'We'll walk you home,' I tell the kid.

Nick realizes there's no point in arguing. If he doesn't soon show up his mother will have a fit of some kind, flying or otherwise.

Nick grudgingly leads Gaffer out the front door ahead of me and onto the sidewalk. The first patch of grass we come across Gaffer circles, squats, and does his business. It's left to me to pick up the pieces. I've had considerable practice.

Nick is back in his lawful home. Gaffer is back in his, lying grudgingly on the living room rug, resigned to the fact his master won't be going upstairs to bed any time soon.

I'm on my third pour of Lagavulin. The bottle has one more it can offer up.

What's with a woman who once filled a fellow's life, who now fills someone else's in record time? What's with someone who couldn't wait to pull back the sheet and have the other side of the bed reheated before it ever got the chance to go cold?

Not that we could have restarted the marriage. That was never going to happen. Truth be told, once we got past the custody circus, we were both bloody relieved it was over.

So, why all this shit about Olsen?

The comeback requires a particularly stiff shot of Scotch.

I said it before, I'll say it again. The prick is too big in his self. He's too bloody cocksure, and in more ways than one.

As subtle as shit that he works out. I've had the piss-poor luck of seeing him in a t-shirt. One look and you know right away he moves weights around like he's bloody well got nothing better to do. My bet is he's older than I am for fuck's sake.

Don't get me wrong. I'll give the asshole credit. He's built to bloody last.

I hate gyms. I hate punishing it out on machines next to some freakin sweathead who thinks he's training for the Olympics. I hate the thought of soaping up in a gym shower with a gut that's still a gut, while around me is a fucking pretentious squad of aging sixpacks.

I once had it figured Olsen stays in shape because his job depends on it. Hang around a cop station and that notion soon goes out the window. No, the inspector works out because he actually gets off on forcing his body into man primordial, ancient hunter-gatherer, naked but for a strip of animal hide.

Fact: all men have these fantasies. The smart ones suck it up.

Alexander Skarsgård playing Tarzan for one. Skarsgåd had a stint at being muscle on a stick. Now he's gone back to looking normal. Schwarzenegger, on the other hand, looks at himself in the mirror and says he wants to vomit. Arnold, get over it for fuck's sake, you're not twenty any more, you stopped being Mr. Universe fifty freakin years ago.

Cocksure Olsen is not going to get over it anytime soon.

Hours later I wake up on the couch with a thick, numbing headache. Gaffer is curled around my legs and it takes me an eye-scrunching several minutes to untangle myself and get my feet to the floor.

Shit. I look across at the empty Lagavulin bottle and have a bleary answer to my brain trauma. Tell me I have more sense than that.

There's a distant determination to get past this and overhaul myself. Somewhere in the future there's an ill-defined corner to be turned.

Right now, I just need to get something in my gut and hope it will dissipate the Scotch. While I stand and wait for the slice of bread to pop up as dry, absorbent toast, I scan my phone.

Shit. Shit. A reminder of a doctor's appointment in an hour. My head hammers with the effort it takes to decide if I should cancel it. Can I pull myself together in less than sixty minutes?

Questionable. But I should try at least. It's a routine follow-up to the tests I had as part of a yearly physical. It won't take more than ten minutes. I can fake normalcy for ten minutes.

I've only just bitten into the toast when my phone rings. Unknown overseas number, it warns me. I'm psyched to give a telemarketer five seconds of my time before jabbing him to silence.

'Hello.' Calm, cool, just in case.

'Sebastian Synard, is that you?'

Only one person does that to my name.

'Gabriela. You're calling from Mexico?'

'*Sí*. From San Miguel.'

'How good to hear your voice.'

Small talk follows, by which time I have had a chance to sit down and refocus, into something that resembles the sharp mind of a private investigator.

'I have a proposition,' she says.

I'm all ears, or as many as I can muster.

'You come to San Miguel. See for yourself what Antonio is up to. You see he arranged the killer. I pay the whole...how you say...shebang.'

Putting "shebang" aside for the moment, this is a lot to put my throbbing head around on short notice. She can sense I'm hesitating.

'Sebastian, you want to find the killer? You think I'm crazy?'

'No, Gabriela, you're not...crazy.'

'Thank you.'

'It's just that it's all so sudden. I need time to think about it.'

'We have no time. Antonio cover up his tracks like mad. You stay with me. I say you are a new friend from Canada. Antonio have no suspicions.' There is a single-minded pause. 'I make it worth your while.'

Interesting. There is a pause on my part, less single-minded. But I need time. 'Can I get back to you?'

'No.'

What's with this "no"? Of course I need time. I can't just fly to Mexico on her whim. I need to know it is worth the effort, that it won't be a pointless wild goose chase that will cut into my valuable time.

'*Very* worth your while.'

Yes, and I'm a sucker for innuendo. But Gabriela, darling, don't be thinking I can be so easily played with.

'What is it? Either you come or I fire you now and go to your policemen.'

My neck stiffens, choking off any response. Stunned, if not surprised.

Predictability has not been Gabriela's strong suit. I figure she is playing a game. Yet I'm not sure I can chance it.

'Let me think.' An intentional few moments of silent pondering to reestablish my professionalism. 'What are my flight options?'

Her tone moderates. 'YYT to YYZ, connecting to MEX."

Is it easier for Gabriela to say YYZ than Toronto? I think not. This woman continues to unbalance me. MEX, I assume, is Mexico City.

'When do you want me there?'

'You leave tomorrow.'

'Gabriela, it's not that easy...'

'We have a saying in México. *Camarón que se duerme se lo lleva la corriente.*

'Really?' If I could spell it I would run it through Google Translate. To save myself the embarrassment that is sure to follow.

'It means "The shrimp that falls asleep is swept away by the current."'

Not so bad. Esoteric little Mexican expression. I let it pass. What it has to do with me I'll never know.

'In other words,' she adds, 'you snooze, you lose.'

In terms of succinctness, it's obvious English leaves Spanish in the dust.

On the positive side, heat this time of the year might do me good. The temperature outside has sunk to single digits. Snow is preparing itself for attack. A few days in the sun of México... margarita, fajita, *señorita*...All expenses paid. Is there a choice?

'You leave YYT at 1230. In twelve hours you arrive MEX. I will be waiting for you at the Airport Hilton. In the morning we drive to San Miguel. There it is. Simple as *tarta de manzana*.'

'*Mañana*.' I'm feeling Mexican already.

The doctor's appointment comes as a relief. The inevitable wait to be called is a chance to further detox myself with Gatorade. Rehydrate and pump in the electrolytes. My personal favourite hangover treatment: Riptide Rush, the frosty, purple one. Believe me, there is no true cure except time, but the aptly named Riptide Rush jolts the body into gear.

I have a further half hour of downtime before my name rings across the waiting room, followed by restrained smirks, and in those with the flu, sudden muffled bursts of coughing.

He is known as Doctor Frank to his long-term patients. Used with affection, but we like how it squares with his bedside manner. The good doctor has been covering all my medical bases since my relocation into St. John's these many healthy years ago. I help the process along by having annual check-ups and blood tests. To date, flying colours on the PSA, EKG, Hep C, flu shot, and stool sample.

Which causes a certain amount of unease when I discover that Doctor Frank's usual jovial nature is noticeably muted.

'I'm going to be honest, Sebastian.'

Never a good start. 'I know, I could do with losing a few pounds.' His annual pronouncement. I thought I'd save him the trouble.

'That's part of it.' He pauses. Also not good. 'In a nutshell, I would now officially classify you as pre-diabetic.'

The word "diabetic" sends my already malfunctioning mind into a further tangle. "Pre-." I hang onto "pre-."

'Continue on this path and you could well end up not being able to wipe your own ass.'

Up to this point I have appreciated his name. Is there any need to flaunt it?

'Crudely put I know.'

'I agree.'

'What you don't seem to agree with is the fact that diabetes has a genetic component. Your mother was diabetic, was she not? And your father?'

Rhetorical, of course. It's in my file. 'And while we're at it, let's toss in Uncle Bill.'

As a good doctor should, he adds a new note to the file. He closes the file and places it on his desk. 'Your blood sugar level is up. Your A1C is now at 6.0.'

A year ago it was 5.5. I remember that because, believe it or not, A1C also happens to be the first half of my postal code and the pair of digits has a nice synchronicity. I digress.

'Below 5.7 is considered normal. At 6.5 you're a type 2 diabetic, which could lead to heart attack or stroke.'

Hence the potential problem with toilet paper usage.

No denying I'm gutted. Doctor Frank may be overstating his case, but, then again, maybe not. Pulsating red light. 'So I should knock off a few pounds.'

'Twenty. At least.'

Covert grimace.

'More exercise. Healthier food. And, given the odour, knock

off the whisky before you get to the point of spilling it on yourself.'

I look down at the shirt I didn't have time to change before racing off to the appointment. I'm not easily embarrassed, but at this point my control mechanisms falter.

'See me in six weeks.' He writes out a requisition for more blood work. 'Get tested a couple of days before you come in. Let's see if whatever diet you come up with is working.'

"Diet." The word immediately puts a bad taste in my mouth.

Doctor Frank smiles and stands up, a reminder he has more patients in need of blunt analysis. He shakes my hand ahead of me going through the door. 'You can do it, Sebastian. Willpower works wonders.'

Such a supportive man, Doctor Frank. I feel the love.

I refuse the word "diet." It's so guilt-ridden. What I'm in need of is a "regime." That's all I have time to decide, given the rush I'm in before flying to Mexico. The good news is I don't have much time to eat. I feel lighter already.

Foremost among the immediate tasks—finding a place for Gaffer to reside while I'm gone. Samantha sucks at inconvenience on short notice, especially since I'll be gone several days, and she's only just come off a stint of having the mutt stay over.

I do have alternate plans for Gaffer but there's no doubt Nick will figure he's the one who should be taking care of business. I'll let him test the water.

I shot Nick an email in the waiting room of the doctor's office, to alert him to my travel plans. I didn't mention Gaffer. That way I can plead innocent when Samantha attacks.

I'm heavy into disinterring summer clothes and sporting them in front of a mirror, deciding which ones keep my gut in check, when I hear Nick inside the front door and Gaffer frantic with affection.

'Tomorrow you're back with me again, Gaff boy!' The dog noses him even more.

Really? 'Your mother's okay with that?'

He looks up. 'Yep. We got her convinced.'

'I haven't talked to her.'

'Fred and me.'

Fred?

Then it dawns on me. He means Frederick.

'He wants me to call him Fred,' Nick says sheepishly.

Fred is it? 'Yesterday you hated him.' Go figure.

Nick stands up. 'Mom didn't want Gaffer staying with us again, but he talked her into it.'

The kid played right into Olsen's hands. Sold his self-respect for dog time.

'That's good.' I try to sound pleased. 'Just remember he's not your father.'

That's not so good. Nick looks at me, his lips tightening, his eyes about to water.

'Sometimes you say the dumbest things.' He's holding it in for all he's worth.

'I'm sorry. You're right. It was dumb.'

'You like it better when I hate him.'

'No, I don't.'

'Yes, you do. You like it better when he says stuff that pisses me off.'

The last thing I want is an argument, with me about to fly off. I pull Nick into me and hug him hard. Shit.

Here is where I should say something about how much I love him. Which I don't because I'm afraid he'll take it the wrong way, like I'm only saying it to get back on his good side. I just hug him for longer and draw his head into my chest.

'You're getting taller, pal. Soon you'll be whipping up there past your old dad.'

Shit. That sounds worse.

Now he can't get back to himself. He plays with Gaffer for a while and I make some hot chocolate for both of us. I give him a kid-friendly version of the phone call with Gabriela and why I'm going to Mexico. He expects to be kept in the loop. It helps in one way, not so much in another.

'I've heard stories about Mexico. Gangs and shoot-outs,' he says. 'You being careful?'

'I trust Gabriela. She'll look out for me.' A lame attempt at reassuring him.

'You don't know what you're getting into. It could be a trap.'

'Listen, Nick man, nothing's going to happen. San Miguel is full of tourists all having a good time. UNESCO World Heritage Site.' I scour my brain to recall what else I picked up on the Google search. 'Oh, yes, voted the best city in the world for travellers by *Travel & Leisure Magazine*.' That should ease his mind. 'Two years in a row.'

'Text me every day.'

'I promise.'

It's getting late. He should be heading home. 'I'll give you a ride.'

'I'd rather walk.'

Normally it would be hell to get him out the door. Not tonight.

'See ya tomorrow, pal. I'll drop Gaffer off on my way to the airport.'

'See ya.' A weak attempt at a hug on his part. I reciprocate with something twice as hard.

A quick turn and he's gone. Even Gaffer is not impressed.

Worry about Nick prods me awake in the middle of the night. When I finally give up trying to get back to sleep, I flip the lid on my laptop and type in "how to lose twenty pounds fast." It's a sombre process, wading past the pictures of junk food I'm expected to vilify. They make me hungry. I persist and eventually narrow my search down to two scenarios, neither one of which is helped by the fact I love Mexican food.

The final, weighty decision is made in the lounge of the St. John's International Airport, as I am about to depart on the 1230 flight to YYZ, connecting for a scheduled arrival of 2230 in MEX.

I have decided on "the dietary strategy," "the eating pattern," "the meal-timing schedule" known as…(drum roll)… Intermittent Fasting!

Acronym: IF. Meaning *if* I can stick with it, *if* I don't slide off the rails partway through, then, according to what I've read, I'll drop the big 2-0 within three months, sending type 2 diabetes permanently out the bathroom window. Bring it on.

There are a number of different ways to tackle IF, depending on what "the regime man" (my choice of words) thinks he can handle. I opt for the 16/8 method: sixteen hours of fasting, followed by a window of eight hours for consumption. Not as hard as it sounds considering the regime man is asleep for a good stretch of the sixteen. It means skipping breakfast, taking the first moderate, but not austere, meal at 1 p.m. and a second in the evening, shutting her down at 9 with a single malt. A piece of the proverbial cake.

And I have to say IF starts out very well. What Air Canada has on its meal menu lends itself to moderation. The Glenlivet does go down nicely, despite being a bit on the tame side. After 2100, zero calories, zilch. Not so much as a whiff of pretzel.

When the flight lands in MEX I'm feeling taut.

8

THERE IS SOMETHING altogether energizing about going from a city of 120,000 to a metropolis of 20,000,000. Going from a brisk 8°C to a balmy 24. From a sweater and puffy jacket to a pale-yellow polo shirt with a discreet bottle of hot sauce embroidered on the pocket. I step outside the terminal and feel the tumult.

I'm hoofing it with only carry-on, which ups the energy level even more. As agreed, I sent Gabriela a text when the flight landed. Her directions to the Airport Hilton are English-as-a-second-language terse and, except for a slip into *nos vemos pronto* at the end, nothing that I don't follow with sustained confidence. I grind to a halt in the hotel lobby within twenty minutes.

'Sebastian, darling.'

I don't recall us being on such promising terms. It deserves a tasteful hug. Reciprocated by the waft of some seemingly expensive perfume.

'We're all checked in. Let's go for a nightcap before we make ourselves comfortable.'

Yes, let's. I look forward to comfortable.

The bar's take on a martini is of course made with tequila.

Together with vermouth, orange bitters, lemon, and jalapeño. Not my idea of a martini, but then again I would rather be drinking Scotch. In either case, an abrupt end to the first day of fasting. You do what you can do. Gabriela takes priority.

Her immediate attention on Antonio makes the martini go down no easier. 'After tomorrow we see my sister. I introduce you into the family. You do your investigator thing and when Antonio shows up, boom, you are on top of the situation.'

The "boom" sets up expectations. Not particularly attainable ones, but outright expectations nonetheless. Gabriela is expecting my PI radar to kick in, leading me to evidence that ties Antonio to the murder. A tall order for someone showing up in Mexico for the first time. Let's hope they speak English.

If I'm feeling intimidated then I'm hell-bent on not letting it show. But equally hell-bent on not letting my guard down. If Antonio arranged a killer once, there'd be nothing stopping him from doing it a second time, should he figure I've stuck my nose where it doesn't belong.

In the meantime there's the matter of getting comfortable.

Gabriela doesn't waste time on preliminaries. The wide-open washroom door while she's in the shower would be my first clue. Following round one, the second would be her decision not to bother with anything except make-up before taking to the king-sized bed. She gives a foreigner a wide playing field to be sure, and if I'm not comfortable by the third round then there's no hope for me.

I sleep like *el niño*, a baby after a whirlwind.

The drive from Mexico City will take about three hours. Her vehicle: an orange metallic BMW Cabriolet.

'Sunset orange metallic,' she notes after catching my admiring scan of the convertible. Either way, that's a lot of tequila.

It takes me a while to settle in. (Convertibles are not something you see much of in Newfoundland, considering a sane owner gets to drive with the top down at most two months of the year.) We're heading north on the 57D, with the surroundings changing from urban sprawl to something less populated, but which I would hesitate to call scenic.

That is, until we approach San Miguel de Allende—spread pleasingly over a high plateau ringed by a range of low mountains, with the core of the old city defined by the soaring, neo-Gothic towers of its landmark church. Exactly like Wikipedia led me to expect.

'*La Parroquia*,' she declares. "One of the most special churches in all México. Now you say it, *La Parroquia*.'

No need for the flash of ego, Gabriela. I saw enough of that last night. Furthermore, I am quite capable of saying the two words, as I demonstrate.

'Close. *La Parroquia*.'

I smile and turn attention elsewhere. 'Is that where you live, in the city centre?'

'*Centro*, no, too many *turistas*.'

'Where then?'

'You will see.' It is becoming increasingly clear that Gabriela relishes the element of surprise.

The city is made up of *colonias*. She is talking neighbourhoods. 'This is San Antonio,' she says, approaching it. 'You know, in English you say Saint Anthony.'

Yes, I do know. 'We have a St. Anthony in Newfoundland. Except people who live there call it *Sin Antny*.' I'm chuckling. 'Newfoundlanders tend not to waste syllables.'

Completely lost on her. 'The city in Texas.' She says it again, slower this time. 'San An-ton-io.'

Rather than dwell on her condescension, I embrace the ambiance—the sun, the sky, the architecture, the noontime flurry of people about the constricted sidewalks.

Gabriela has her way of negotiating the narrowing streets that involves suppressed irritation, interspersed with abbreviated hand gestures. The Cabriolet curbs her enthusiasm. If she didn't have an open-air audience who knows how much louder she would have shouted '*Eres tan pendejo!*' Whatever that means. Nothing good I'm sure.

'Asshole!' she shouts to relieve my uncertainty.

The asshole turns right and we are left with the street to ourselves. I have yet to see a front yard. I can only assume there are residences behind the façades that butt up against the sidewalks. Heavy wooden doors are a big clue.

We slow down. In the case of Gabriela's residence, there's also a garage door that opens to allow the Cabriolet to edge inside, inches to spare. The door closes behind us, together with the world outside. We step into Gabriela's private enclave, starting with an interior courtyard, replete with planted palms, brightly patterned terracotta floor tiles, and a nest of modish rattan furniture. I recognize it from the online picture, minus the tequila and lounging attire.

I'm feeling overdressed. I need time to unwind after the long drive. A little lunch, a drink of some exotic design. An hour to relax and collect myself before we venture out again into the real world.

Once I'm past the glass door into the house, my impression of Gabriela's lifestyle expands exponentially. The interior is laden with designer taste, a coordinated mix of Mexican and ultra-modern. Chic without betraying her heritage.

High ceilings and expansive walls bear oversize paintings that coordinate with the colours of the walls and sofas remarkably well. Scattered about the floor and shelves are what I take to be Mexican folk art, all of it attention-getting. All likely to be worth a lot, though I have no way of knowing.

She attempts to amplify my awe. She indicates one particular painting, high on a far wall. The whimsical, jewel-tone imagery is striking in its detail, the swirling figure at its centre looking like a character out of *Cirque du Soleil*.

'This is Toller Cranston.'

The Canadian figure skater? World famous when I was a kid. Olympic medalist. 'Are you sure? The face doesn't look like his.'

'*Idiota*,' she mutters, in jest certainly. 'The painter, not the person in the picture.'

How was I to know that when Toller Cranston retired from skating he moved to San Miguel to paint. Lived here until he passed away suddenly a few years ago.

She looks up again at the painting. 'You like it?'

'It's different.'

That's obviously not enough to satisfy her. Gabriela likes to be satisfied.

'Extraordinary in so many ways,' I add.

That's better. At least she is smiling, if indulgently.

Thankfully there's lots more of the house begging for attention. It's angled and showy, with a bank of tall windows that overlook the courtyard. The upstairs rooms are as thick with arty detail as the main floor. All a bit over the top, to my mind, but that thought I keep to myself.

Her bedroom suite is the *pièce de résistance*. A prodigious chandelier hangs over the voluminous bed, an exploding cluster of three-dimensional stars made from pierced tin plates.

'Tin art is a speciality in San Miguel. Beautiful, isn't it? Fifteen stars. Fifteen is my lucky number.'

No doubt the bed has seen more than a few opportunities for Gabriela to try her luck. Just saying, not throwing any stones.

Gabriela's housekeeper has arrived, realigning our thoughts to something more virtuous. Gabriela introduces her as Josefina, then proceeds to call her Josie.

Josie is not the least bit surprised by my presence in the

house, which reinforces my assumptions about Gabriela and lucky numbers. Josie's English is close to non-existent so there is a lot of smiling and nodding on my part as she and Gabriela banter on in animated Spanish. The offshoot is a hastily prepared lunch for the two of us in the courtyard, while flamenco music plays in the background.

It would seem flamenco is another of Gabriela's passions. It is hard to keep up. I know nothing of flamenco and would have expected it to remain that way for the rest of my life. Gabriela, I sense, has other plans.

'Tomorrow we'll get down to business. Today you get to know my city.'

It's a fifteen-minute walk to *El Centro*, over the somewhat flat, and definitely uneven stones that make up the narrow sidewalks. Ah, the famous "jerky" stones, incentive for sprained ankles. Careful ambling (ah, to avoid jerking about I see) is in order. The streets are a melange of colonial façades in earthy yellow, ochre, and tangerine, with the occasional swath of turquoise and pink. Brings to mind some streets in downtown St. John's, except it's stucco, not wood; in sunshine, not fog.

At the core of *El Centro* is *El Jardín*, a centuries-old plaza, defined by large, manicured trees, broad borders of shrubs and flowers and criss-crossing paths shaped by patterned flagstone. Gabriela locks her arm into mine and leads me to one of the numerous wrought iron benches.

I'm looking across a flurry of pedestrians and skyward. 'Ah, *La Parroquia*.' I have been practicing.

'Very close.' She edges tighter to me, her skirt creeping immodestly thighward. I have trouble concentrating on the main attraction of this UNESCO World Heritage Site. The Tablelands it's not.

Gabriela seems to be finding it all intrinsically romantic. Which, were I to think about it for long, would surprise me since she must have lingered in this plaza hundreds of times. I choose not to think about it any longer. Embrace the moment, let the Mexican sun beam down and warm my skeptical soul. Let the music brush the nastiness of the world aside for the moment. It will reappear soon enough.

The music in question emanates from a mariachi band, six *señors* in black suits bedecked with elaborate silver buttons and wide bands of thick silver embroidery. The dazzle covers much of the jacket and straight down the leg of the pants to the heavily tooled boots. And sombreros—magnificently gaudy, super wide-rimmed sombreros that would be a great curiosity to behold from a distance.

Unfortunately by the time I'm done hoping they will walk past, they have surrounded us in a semi-circle, instruments at the ready. As I have belatedly figured out, they stroll about the plaza on the lookout for potential mariachi enthusiasts willing to offer money for a song, in the process drawing the eyes and ears of everyone within gawking distance.

If not me, then Gabriela fits the profile of mariachi zealot. She senses my discomfort and nudges me. 'Don't be a sourcat.'

Me, a sourcat? I endure the manly option, and pretend I'm enjoying the sudden attention.

Gabriela has a request. Should I be surprised? Apparently a favourite. 'My first boyfriend used to sing it to me.'

In that case, a song that has stood the test of time. I have zero chance of guessing what it might be, given that I know little about Mexican culture, beyond what I can fork into my mouth.

Strike up the band and let's get my embarrassment over with. Here they are, ready to go—trumpet, violin, accordion, guitar. And two guitar lookalikes, one undersized, the other well oversized, no doubt each with some curious name I wouldn't be able to pronounce no matter how hard I'd try. Let's get on with it.

The instruments strike an energetic burst of chords. Gabriela's rear is already bouncing off the park bench.

> '*Para bailar La Bamba*
> *Para bailar La Bamba*
> *Se necessita una poca de gracia*
> *Una poca de gracia*
> *Para mi, para ti, ay arriba, ay arriba…*'

Jesus.

My parents loved Ritchie Valens. I loved Los Lobos. Back in the days.

There's no likelihood I'm going to resist when Gabriela grabs my hand and pulls me to my feet. She's gyrating about the flagstone with abandon, as if the music has triggered a release she's been craving for days. I'm no match for her, but I'm no stick-in-the-mud either. And, what the hell, I throw in a few butt shakes of my own.

The mariachi boys are loving it, and spread themselves wide so more of the crowd can take in the action.

> '*Yo no soy marinero*
> *Yo no soy marinero, soy capitan*
> *Soy capitan, soy capitan!*'

Whoa, if she wants me to be the captain, I'll be the captain. '*Bam-ba, bamba!*' I'm singing out, if lost in the chorus of voices surrounding us. '*Bam-ba, bamba! Bam-ba, bamba!*'

On the last strike of the guitar strings Gabriela and I collapse on the park bench to wild applause. Whoa, let me congratulate myself on rising to the occasion. I wrap an arm around Gabriela and plant a kiss on her cheek. She reciprocates two-fold. Her effervescence subsides long enough to search for money to pay the jocular band of musicians. I offer an opened wallet. Her beautifully manicured nails emerge with a 500-peso bill.

I have only a vague notion of what that translates to in Canadian dollars, but the musicians are all smiles. I like the idea of leaving a trail of goodwill throughout the city.

By the time we reach our final stop, the trail is a lengthy one and my wallet is empty. To be refurbished in the morning at the nearest ATM.

Ah, but money well spent. We've sipped cortados at *Ki'bok*, lingered over cocktails and tapas on the rooftop at *El Luna*, wined and dined at *La Única*, wrapped ourselves in the art of flamenco at *El Tupinamba*. Gabriela is a woman who likes her amenities. Not a cheap date, but then again she's paying the whole "shebang" otherwise. So no complaints, even as I wonder how many trips to the trough my bank account can endure.

The night of course doesn't end there. The football field of a bed under the tin-holed starburst provides a fitting closure. If we are both a bit drunk from the copious number of beverages that passed our lips over the course of the city tour, it doesn't show. At least, I'm thinking it doesn't show. I'm thinking we brought things to a climax, but my recollection could be somewhat blurred.

When we come to life in the morning, there is a sizable gap between us. We seemed to have cocooned ourselves on opposite sides of the bed. Gabriela slips out and into the shower, this time with the door noticeably shut.

When she re-enters the room she's all business. 'The shower is free,' she announces unnecessarily. She ups the dimmer switch so the starburst convulses the room with light.

Before she turns even more directive, I slip my legs to the carpet and head slowly to the bathroom, my balance slightly out of whack. I'm halfway there before it registers that I'm doing a full frontal. I smile. I'm good for it.

She stops brushing her hair and peers at me. But not in the manner I would have hoped. In a manner that suggests she's inserting me into her ranking of all the men who have previously emerged from between her sheets. Her intake of breath tells me I'm somewhere on the lower level of her titillation bar graph.

It stirs my manhood, metaphorically.

I stop and stare back. 'The tequila fucked me up.' It just sort of erupted, kind of like the starburst.

She doesn't quite know what to say. She refrains from defending the honour of her prized liquor, and instead turns aside and resumes brushing her hair. I've touched a nerve, but not one that was raw enough for her to retaliate.

As for me, the slap of water in the shower brings me back to life. The trail of soap down the chest and over the gentle curve of stomach smartens me up. I regret blurting out an insult to what has allowed her to bring me to Mexico free of charge, gut or no gut.

When I re-enter the room, this time banded by a towel, I'm prepared to apologize. But Gabriela appears to have put it out of her mind. She's wedged herself into a pair of jeans, donned a silky top, and done something interesting to her hair. She's smiling and eager to start our day.

'I'll be in the kitchen. Double espresso for you?'

IF permits black (calorie-free) coffee in the fasting period. Thankfully. The jolt of caffeine is manna from heaven. As for the actual manna, the sweet bread pastries that Josie arrives with and lays on the counter between us, they are out of the question.

'*Pan dulce*,' says Gabriela, directing her manicured nails towards the delicacies. 'Go ahead have one. Josie brought them especially for you.'

'*Sí*,' says the housekeeper, eagerly.

I look at the array as if I'm having second thoughts. 'No,

really. Thank you all the same.' I smile at a Josie, and then at Gabriela, as a way of offering my regrets. 'I'm on a…well…a regime.'

"Regime" is not in Gabriela's English vocabulary.

'My doctor tells me I need to lose a little weight.'

Gabriela, who has already bitten into a small, shell-shaped *pan dulce*, smiles. 'Go ahead, have one. Josie will be insulted.'

'*Sí*,' says Josie, who I am sure doesn't have a sweet clue what is being debated.

A regime debate, one of many in the coming weeks I'm sure. Do I stand my ground and look petty? Or take one and blow the regime for the day? I take note of Josie's firm anticipation, and opt for the latter. I route my fingers to the smallest *pan dulce*, take a bite, fending off their disapproval.

'*Buena, sí?*' says Josie.

'*Sí*.' I take another bite, and another, until it has been consumed.

Hardly a good start to the day, but as the day is about to ramp up, I have the feeling that the guilt of eating a *pan dulce* before the anointed end to the fasting period will become the least of my concerns.

The prospect of meeting Simón's mother and the dark demon of a stepfather, Antonio, clears my mind as we drive to their property on the outskirts of San Miguel.

'He's a fucking dog of a man.'

Gabriela's terse analysis cuts through the last bit of morning lethargy. I feel I should be preparing for a rabies shot.

The driveway leading to their house is a long one, defined on both sides by a landscape of heavy equipment, set behind parallel lines of palm trees that do nothing but confirm the image I have of Antonio as a tough guy all about making money. Still, a PI learns to reserve judgment until actually meeting the suspect. I set Gabriela's dog reference aside.

Rosa, Simón's mother and Gabriela's older sister, we meet first, outside the front entrance of the sprawling house.

Rosa embraces me as if I were Simón's much-cherished friend. I have no idea what Gabriela has told her about me, and because her English is restricted to a few heavily accented words, I suspect I'll never get the full story.

There are some hints. Once she gives up on wrapping her Spanish tongue around my surname, she decides to stick with *Sebastián*. I rather like the Spanish cadence, but then, as if it were a bit too familiar, she begins addressing me as *el profesor*.

Gabriela catches my eye and winks. A very subtle wink accompanied by an equally subtle touch of a smile, neither for Rosa's consumption.

Let sleeping dogs lie. My considered opinion. If, in Gabriela's mind, it gives me cover, then it may indeed prove useful.

In any case Rosa thinks nothing of it. She is still in mourning for her son, and is too much into the process of pulling her life back together to be in need of anything but fond memories of Simón. These I can provide. Nothing I personally experienced of course, but plenty to pass on from the students who were his friends.

I talk, Gabriela translates. I have no way of knowing how accurate she's being but whatever she's saying it seems to be helpful to Rosa. When I'm through, I'm so bold as to give her a hug.

Antonio arrives to find me embracing his wife.

Antonio is all of 5' 4. If I thought I could get away with it unnoticed, I would do a double take. He does compensate by being built like a bear. A juvenile bear, but a bear nonetheless. His handshake is bear-like as well, so there is the definite indication he stands his ground, as restricted as that ground might be.

Don't get me wrong. Height normally has no bearing on my judgement of my fellow man. My friends span the gamut. So why had I expected Antonio to spread to at least six feet? Only because it's natural to picture dogged evildoers as towering over you rather than making direct eye contact with your Adam's apple.

Gabriela senses my surprise, but appears to like the fact it adds to the intrigue. She lets Antonio have his moment, but then injects herself prominently in the scene. 'Antonio,' she booms, and sure of his attention, lowers the decibels. 'Sebastian is a friend I met in Canada. He wanted to visit me. Canada is so cold this time of the year.'

'I have friends from Canada.' Antonio speaks English as well as Gabriela, and with more confidence, if volume is an indication. 'They come here because no snow to shovel. I build them houses with long driveways.'

He doesn't crack a smile. I wouldn't list a sense of humour in his personality profile.

I would leave "friendly toward strangers" off the list as well. When Gabriela refers to me as *el profesor*, he laughs.

Laugh you might, short ass, but at least I know what a university looks like. Unlike some.

It is all downhill from there. Antonio is determined to embarrass his wife and Gabriela with his antics, while I do all I can to defend myself without descending to his level.

'Hey, Sebastian. Gabriela likes her men. You no feel you take a number and wait in line?'

'You little prick,' she shouts. 'I'd kick you in the *cojones* if you had any.'

Those pointy-toed shoes of hers, not good on the *cojones* I'm sure. I step in. 'Antonio, man. There's no need...'

'You gutless Canadian, you no tell me what to do. You Canadians play football like shit.'

What the hell?

'You play your soccer like shit. *Eeeh, puto!* Now you understand.'

He's talking like manliness comes down to football. I look at Antonio and the player that storms to mind is Diego Maradona. No taller than Antonio, maybe shorter. And Messi, what 5'7?

Rosa takes charge. '¡*Basta*! Antonio, Gabriela. ¡*Basta*!

It only takes the one word. It would appear that Rosa has had practice at this. The flare of insults is suddenly over.

'*El profesor, sígame por favor.*' She hooks her arm in mine and leads me inside the house. The two others follow dutifully behind.

In the dining room there's a heavy Spanish Colonial table set for four, with a large pitcher of coffee and (what else?) an array of *pan dulce*. I see several I'm willing to try, in celebration of the calm after the storm.

Antonio heads for a particular place at the table. He looks less fierce seated. I'm wondering if his chair sports a cushion.

Gabriela borders on cheerful. She seats herself next to him and the two talk in Spanish and sound reasonably civil. I have the feeling that what I witnessed outside—the reference to Antonio's *cojones*—is a standard routine.

But, then, the civility doesn't last. Insults reignite the conversation, in English and on the fringes of Rosa's hearing. Antonio mutters an outrageous statement, seemingly to inflame Gabriela. She peers at him as if he were an idiot, then counters with calmly executed abuse to goad him further. Obviously no love lost between the pair, yet they've fashioned a weird truce to keep peace with the matriarchal Rosa.

Antonio appears done with me. Apparently, foreigners who are not football fiends hold little interest for him except as a means of making money. That, or he's tired of Gabriela's steady stream of male companions. (They come, they go, no point in investing in getting to know them.) That, or Antonio is a little bastard. Nonetheless, I'm here to figure him out, to determine if he could, in any way, directly or indirectly, be involved in Simón's demise.

I'm seated opposite him. 'Antonio.' He looks across the table, his eyes angled slightly up, mine down. A compromise and a reasonable entry point. 'I didn't know Simón, but I know his friends. They do not understand why anyone would want to murder him.' I can be this direct because Rosa has no idea what I'm saying, only that I mentioned her son by name.

Antonio says nothing. Gabriela prompts him with an elbow to the shoulder. A snarlish grunt. He glances at Rosa, who is close to tears. What eventually emerges from his lips is anything but venomous.

'Simón and me, we make our blow-ups. Simón—a smart kid but stubborn as hell.' Antonio looks over at Rosa. 'Simón— *un buen hijo.*'

I need to up the stakes. 'You threatened your dogs on him. Your dogs are killers.'

Antonio glances at Rosa again, then leans over the table at me. He takes a breath, and on the exhale, too low for Rosa to hear, 'You Canadian, I feed you to the fucking dogs.' He sits back and smiles at me, then at Rosa.

Up yours, you little bastard. That and a stiff middle finger. I suppress both my gut reactions. My gut churns in silence. I smile dismissively.

Now he's standing away from the table, hardly any taller than when he was sitting down. My smile broadens.

'You want to see my dogs,' he says. 'Come, I show you my dogs.'

'You want to feed me to your dogs?' I ask pointedly.

He laughs. 'Fucking Canadian, you no take the joke. Simón laughed at me. He take the joke.'

The self-satisfied little jerk walks out of the room, expecting me to follow. Gabriela hooks her arm in mine and leans into me. 'The man is a liar and a son-of-a-bitch.' She offers her other arm to Rosa and leans into her. 'Antonio, *él es bueno contigo.*'

Rosa walks with us out the front door, serene and thankful. Gabriela has satiated one of us at least.

The pair of dogs are in an enclosure, some distance away. With Antonio approaching they launch into a chorus of howls and yelps. I have no wish to witness this display of dog frenzy, but Gabriela insists. 'Doberman Pinscher,' she says, not quite getting it right, but nonetheless with unrestrained satisfaction.

The closer we get, the more vicious their canine dispositions. They rail against the chain-link fence, their gaping mouths aimed in my direction, both rows of spiked teeth on full display, fangs that could rip flesh like nobody's business.

Against every effort to play it cool, my spine crawls. Placid, innocent Gaffer seems very far away.

Antonio shouts them down and tosses over the fence a hunk of raw meat to each of the demons. For my benefit undoubtedly. They attack the meat like they would human flesh were it to be sacrificed.

'A treat,' says Antonio. 'It make their blood redded.'

I get the gist. A dirty little smirk has full rein across his face.

'Did Simón enjoy your dogs?'

'Simón hate Antonio's dogs. He hate Antonio more.'

He looks at Rosa but she has no notion what is being said. She's pleased to think her son is being talked about, and in a good way she assumes after Antonio takes her hand and kisses it. The hand doesn't have far to go to reach the lips of the two-faced bantam.

'I no harm a hair on the son of my dear sweet woman.' He kisses her hand again. Then slips his other arm around her shoulder and draws her tight to him. They are roughly the same height.

Is there any more to be said? Not on my part. Nothing that will do any more than confirm what I already know. Antonio is not about to unload another version of himself, one that would clinch the fact he was capable of arranging to have Simón knocked off.

Would he have done it? That's the central question, the one that hangs in the air as Gabriela drives back into San Miguel and to *Hecho en México* for lunch. On the lofty walls of the restaurant's dining room hang several large paintings by the Canadian figure skating champ. Gabriela feels right at home. The staff greet her affectionately, and they chatter in animated Spanish. One of them leads us to her favourite table for two, and slips away the reserved sign.

The *cochinita pibil* tacos are excellent, the conversation not so good.

Gabriela doesn't have to ask the question. I know what's on her mind.

I answer on a positive note. 'He's quite capable of doing it.'

'*Sí, sí*,' she says, embracing my optimism.

I'm afraid it doesn't last. I continue, 'Whether he would is an entirely different question. Honestly, I don't think so. He loves Rosa too much to have her son murdered.'

'You don't know Antonio,' she counters petulantly, as if I had betrayed her. 'I'm not paying you good money to be soft in the heart. You saw his dogs!'

'His dogs are there to intimidate his enemies.'

'He hires men to kill like they are his dogs.'

'You have proof of this?'

'I don't need your proof.'

Gabriela is not thinking straight. Her emotion is getting the better of her. 'We need something substantial if we are going to take this to the police. We need some connection between Antonio in Mexico and the killer in Newfoundland. He obviously didn't hire someone in Newfoundland to do it. He wouldn't have the network to set it up. He would have to have hired someone here, someone who speaks English well, who wouldn't be noticed as a foreigner, someone he could fly to Newfoundland, track down Simón, do the job, then fly back to Mexico without drawing attention to himself. Gabriela, that's a very tall order.'

The conversation continues back at her house. The drive there has given her a chance to put her argument in place.

'Order not so tall. Antonio knows fucking Canadians here. You heard him say. Some bastards like Antonio. Some need money to pay for the big house he builds for them with the long driveway.'

'Gabriela, you're getting carried away.'

'You the one carried away. My mind is right here and I know Antonio.'

'I'm willing to listen.' The least I can do. She's the client after all.

'So he make a deal with some guy. You go to Canada, you do me this favour and your house in San Miguel, it free of charge.'

This is really stretching it. I go along with her, let her get it out of her system. 'Okay, say that's what happens. What's the motive? It's got to be a good one. He thinks the world of Rosa. She thinks the world of him. But now he decides to have her son killed. Why? For what reason would he do that? It better be a good one.'

Gabriela sips her margarita and sets it back on the courtyard table. She looks around to make sure Josie is inside the house, then turns her full expressive face to mine. 'Simón told Antonio he had proof the runt did "sore shin." He threatened to tell the police.'

Sore shin? He kicked people in the shin? Then it clicks in. 'Extortion.'

'Like I said.'

'What, specifically?'

'He bids on contracts, every one, always lowest bid. Then he says to number two bidder, you pay me this money and I take back my bid, I make up story why I no can do the job—no find workers, my equipment break, I too busy. Then number two gets job. Sore shin.'

'Then he kicked him in the shin for good measure?'

She doesn't laugh, which is probably for the best. She stares at me, expecting a reaction to confirm my horror at the revelation.

I wouldn't be surprised, of course, if Antonio did such a thing. 'If he did, and Simón knew it, would Simón really go the police knowing what it would do to his mother? She would be devastated.'

'Simón dead or alive, she devastated. So Antonio thinks him better dead.'

She has a point. I'm still not sure it's the right one. 'Give me some time to think about it.'

'You take time. You think,' she says, staring hard at me. 'I have business to do. I see you in a couple of hours.'

After reworking her makeup and slipping into a different, classier outfit, Gabriela heads off to her tequila marketing job. Her regular life must go on if she's to maintain the lifestyle to which she is accustomed.

With Gabriela out the door and Josie, having finished up for the day, not far behind her, the weight of being a houseguest is lifted. I relish the relative peace and quiet. I stretch out on one of the thickly cushioned chaise lounge chairs and sip on the fruit-filled cocktail Josie made for me as a parting gesture.

It gives me a chance to revisit the morning encounter with Antonio. If my instincts are right and Antonio played no part in Simón's demise, then who in San Miguel did? Maybe no one. Maybe it's all wishful thinking on Gabriela's part. As she sees it, hang out with the wrong people in Mexico and there's a price to pay.

But she has no insight into Simón's other life. His university life, the one he had been living for the past half dozen years. She knows nothing of the people he's encountered, the relationships made and broken, the jealousies unleashed. And she has no idea of what those in the academic world are capable of, when animosities take hold and fester.

Gabriela's determination to pin the murder on Antonio intrigues me. She intrigues me, what little I know of her. With her out of the house, there's the shameless opportunity to find out more. A PI thrives on stealth, especially in an environment so devoid of risk, even if it is aimed at the person who hired you.

I'll give myself an hour, to account for the possibility of an early return. Where to start, the only question. Logically the small office off the kitchen.

I avoid her computer. It will leave traces of someone opening files, and in any case is likely password protected. The desk drawers offer nothing but tequila promotional material and the odds and ends found in any workspace. No leather-tooled address book, as I hoped for, but then paper address books are very old school. There are photos pinned to a corkboard on the opposite wall. Gabriela and clients by the look of it, and a few selfies taken in and out of a pool. Wet breasts bursting out of what little covers them, barely enough to keep me focused on the task at hand.

A deep breath. I don't want to spend too much time in one spot. Better a quick, systematic rummage through several parts of the house. The afternoon presses on, the allotted time wears away, with nothing to show for it. I've deliberately saved the best until last. Even if there is nothing to be found, there's an inherent thrill in frisking her underwear drawer.

I know to carefully survey the arrangement of the contents

before executing the game plan. From my experience, some women (i.e., Samantha) are meticulous in how they go about organizing their lingerie. At first glance, it would appear that Gabriela is less particular. It might have something to do with the sparse amount of fabric used for each item. It's a skimpy free-for-all as far as I can tell. Still, one has to be careful not to dislodge any order that might not be obvious to the naked eye. One hand in and around and under the silky ruffles and strings. The goal is anything that might be lying beneath the throng of thongs. I feel my crotch tightening the deeper I delve.

It might be outdated to think of this as a place for secretive items other than the, ummmm, pocket rocket, which I carefully avoid after first contact, continuing the hand search in the opposite direction. I am about to give up and abruptly terminate my reverie when my fingertips trace over a thin sheath that has the semblance of paper. On further fingertip exploration it appears to be an envelope.

I slip it from its sanctuary under the undies. The letter-size, rose-coloured envelope is hand printed with the words "To Tequila, with Love." Strange. A mix of business and pleasure?

The envelope is unsealed and inside is a sheet of white paper folded twice to fit the envelope. I open it with no notion of what to expect. Could be a useless scrap of trivia.

Or it could be a photograph, computer printed on the upper third of the sheet of paper. An awkward selfie of three people, the colours slightly off. Perhaps the ink cartridge acting up.

To the left, a deliberate, orderly Gabriela. Next to her, Simón, in cap and gown, holding what must be a diploma, rolled and tied with red ribbon. And to the right, one arm around Simón's shoulder, the other outstretched to take the picture, towers the professor from the University of Texas, Troy Foster.

Why hidden? Why not properly printed, framed and on the

dresser? The photo has thrown me off for the moment.

It shouldn't have, when I think about it. It must have been taken at Simón's graduation in the spring. Gabriela attended the ceremony, perhaps in lieu of his mother, for whatever reason. Foster was the proud academic who had guided the gifted protégé through his master's degree.

Neither of them looks particularly upbeat. No prelude to a tossing in the air of the mortar board. Maybe that's what threw me off.

I refold the paper, slip it back in the envelope, and take a deep dive through the underthings, making sure the envelope is positioned exactly as I found it. My hand pauses for only a few pleasurable seconds before emerging and closing the drawer.

The clandestine probe reveals nothing more of note, though it is amazing the amount of tequila Gabriela has stored in one closet or another. Either she stockpiles for quick delivery or she keeps a lot of friends smiling.

She shows up to discover me in the lounge chair deep into note-taking, attempting to connect some of the investigative dots. I've come to some conclusions, one of which is not going to be especially thrilling for Gabriela.

I'm sticking by my doubts that Antonio is the chief suspect. I'm willing to concede a position in the maybe column, but nothing more.

'Who then?' she says, close to pouting. Yes, too used to getting her own way.

She's expecting results. She's paid her money, she wants her answers.

'It all takes time, Gabriela. I can't be rushing to conclusions.'

'You haven't got a clue.'

Her command of English slang is too limited for me to take it as a personal slight. No doubt she means a clue to the identity of the murderer.

'Yes, as a matter of fact, I have an assortment of clues.' Imperative to sound like I'm making progress. A private investigator learns to float ideas, as scattered as they might be, to see where they will take him. So yes, I do have a clue. Yes, in fact, several of them.

She stares at me and fidgets.

'I'm thinking of Troy Foster as a possibility?'

I'm expecting a bit of a stunned response. I'm not far off the mark. Not stunned enough to stop a bilingual torrent of a comeback.

'The *profesor*? The Texas *profesor*? You *loco. Estás lleno de mierda!*'

I know what *merde* is in French. Safe to assume it's not far off the Spanish.

'You know the professor?'

'Of course I know the *profesor*. He visit San Miguel. Simón was his favourite student. He loved Simón. *Estás lleno de mierda!*'

I need to backtrack. I feel dangerously close to being fired. 'Just floating possibilities. Obviously you know him better than I do.'

Just how well, I'm left to wonder. I'm doubtful she could resist trying her luck with the big Texan under the exploding stars.

She calms down, somewhat. Enough that I suggest I take her out for dinner. She plays hard to win back, but finally agrees and struts off to change.

I pay for sending up the trial balloon on Troy Foster. She leads me to *Zumo*, what must be one of the most expensive restaurants in San Miguel. She orders a succession of cocktails and the seven-course tasting menu. With wine pairings. It amounts to another stiff jolt to my credit card.

The atmosphere between the *Tartar de Atún* and the *Filete de Res a la Parrilla* is tense. It does ease with the *Tamal de Chocolate*, and by the time we reach the *Carajillos* (coffee spiked with *Cuarenta y Tres*) the conversation I think resembles normal, whatever normal is between the two of us, which I haven't quite figured out as yet.

Gabriela is impetuous. Her passions turn on a dime. Not great to work for, but once she turns in your favour she's all in, so to speak. By the time we reach home, she's massaging the back of my neck in perfect, guileless rhythm.

The tin-plated stars explode tonight. All fifteen of them at the same time, and some more than once.

Gabriela is an early riser when she wants to be. It's hardly daylight and she returns from the kitchen with a coffee, sitting up in bed shaping and buffing her nails and outlining our plans for the day. She thinks I need time outside the city to "reboot" my mind. I think she means reset my mind to her way of thinking.

'A spa day,' she says. 'I take one every week. You'll love it. Relax. Reboot. Let your body heal.'

I don't think my body is in need of healing. Besides, I'm still half asleep and I'm not a spa kinda guy. Joining an untidy collection of sparsely clad bodies, all coming together to shed their worldly frustrations? Not my idea of relaxation.

She pokes at me with her emery board. An exaggerated groan. Truth is I don't have much choice if I want to stabilize my relationship with Gabriela. She's in need of attention, and given her two-act drama of last evening, it's best if I play by her rules of engagement.

'It's the closest thing we have to a beach.'

San Miguel is inland. It's a seven-hour drive to get to the coast. Soaking in a mineral pool with the option of a massage in a steamy cabana is apparently the only game in town.

'You'll love it.'

I'm sure I will.

By 8 a.m. (yes, 8 a.m.) we have driven the fifteen minutes out of town and arrive at the spa.

La Gruta, the sign says. The Grotto, says Google Translate. Really? The Grotto.

We exit the Cabriolet, just as *La Gruta* opens. We're their first spa fanatics for the day. After I don trunks and turn the key on my clothes and valuables in a locker, I psyche myself up for a religious conversion of some variety.

I emerge onto the spa-scape in a rented terrycloth robe and sunglasses. A robust breath, a readiness to embrace the day. The fractured early morning rays have given way to brilliant sunshine. It is a boost to conversion.

'What do you think?'

It's Gabriela, her robe agape and her tanned, bikinied public exposure looking very good for this early hour. It is at times like these, rare though they are, that I wish my eggshell white hide had experienced more sun. The contrast with Gabriela would be too hard on the eyes and ego, so I make the decision to remain tightly robed until such time as I take to the water.

'How about a cappuccino?' I propose, sidelining my dietary regime yet again.

The outdoor restaurant kiosk is just being unshuttered as we arrive. The staff all know Gabriela and she embraces their goodwill, if a bit impatiently. As for me, I would appear to be the flavour of the month. Or perhaps week. It's hard to tell.

The cappuccino serves its purpose. It offsets the pain in the butt of being a spa alien. I smile. Gabriela smiles.

The moment doesn't last. Gabriela is anxious to get started. She has a routine, in which I will partake in good humour, and pretend enthusiasm. PI professionalism.

There are several pools of various configurations. And there is indeed a grotto, which Gabriela leads me to first. Early birds that we are, we'll have it all to ourselves, she notes expectantly. As if I need additional reason to shed the robe, hang it on a hook in the designated area, and descend the steps and into the pool.

My entrance unfolds without comment. Gabriela is being charitable, in contrast to her outburst the day before.

The grotto is man-made. We wade through waist-high water along a narrow passageway, flanked by fake craggy rock that's been painted white and dimly lit. Gabriela is in no hurry, preferring to bob along, the blue-green water cascading from her neck down and over her bountiful, skimpily covered breasts. It does give a lift to the spa experience.

In fact the tunnel ends before I realize it, giving way to a step up and over a ledge and then a few more steps down to a wide, circular pool that appears to have a central fountain spewing a curtain of water. It's hard to tell, even after I slip my sunglasses to the top of my head. The pool is spot-lit underwater.

All very atmospheric. All very sensual. A retreat Gabriela relishes, given the way she slithers about the water.

She extends her hand and draws me toward a niche in the rock wall. With her back to the wall she slides her hands over my buttocks and gathers me into that ample chest. My hold on the myth of a lame spa experience disintegrates.

She's all over me. Now insisting I turn my back to her so she can massage my neck and shoulders. But, given the length of her nails, it turns out to be not quite the erotic experience I was anticipating.

She senses my discomfort and slides her hands along my shoulders and down my upper arms. Much better. Her hands veer to my midriff. I wince. Not the place to linger.

She grabs onto the excess gut and drives her fingernails into it. Fuck.

Another pair of hands, thick and stubby, latch onto my throat. Holy fuck!

I twist about uselessly. The sunglasses go flying. Gabriela slips away.

The hands jerk tighter! I gasp for breath. Some unseen fucker is strangling me. Gabriela calls out what sounds like, 'Let him go. Let him go.' Hard to tell with my head under fucking water.

Survivor instincts kick in! I've bloody well watched the PI course videos!

Forget the hands around the throat. Use the free limbs.

Elbow rammed into the fucker's gut! Foot smashed down on the fucker's instep! Leg bent and kicked back and up!

Heel right into the soft dangly bits inside his trunks! Leg didn't have far to go. He's a short little fucker whoever he is.

His grip on my neck goes weak. My head pops above the surface, air surges into my lungs. In a mad panic I lunge away from the two of them. Across the pool, up the steps, over the ledge, into the tunnel! Arms flying down and through the water to thrust me forward even more.

I don't look behind. There's one goal—end of the tunnel and out of the water.

I grab the robe from its hook, race over the lawn, dodge around those just arriving for the day, all the time working my way into the robe and searching its pockets to find the locker key.

I fumble the key into the lock, haul the door open and grab everything I see. Race out of the locker room and past the front desk, robe still wide open, flying past the people lined up to check in.

Just as I reach the outside a taxi pulls up and parks at the end of the laneway. Two kids and a mother pile out one side. I pile into the other.

'Mexico City,' I croak. 'Airport.'

The driver turns, startled. Either at the sight of me, or his luck to get a three-hour fare. 'You dress first?'

'Get me the hell out of here,' I croak again.

He doesn't argue. We're gone, the chaotic path behind me.

I rub my throat and breathe. And breathe some more, thanking whatever blessed powers for good just saved me.

Only then is there time for some wave of understanding to catch up. The runt wanted me dead? What the hell. Antonio? If not his own stubby hands, then those of a hired runt.

And Gabriela? Could it be that a second runt grabbed her and dragged her away from me while the first was getting his balls walloped?

Nothing is for sure except that when my throat recovers I'll have the last laugh. Laced with the emotion of knowing that had the bastard been bigger and tougher I might have been left a floating corpse.

I'm slouched in the back seat, unable to hold back the dread of Nicholas being left without me. Damn close to tears. Choking them back hurts like hell.

'You okay?' the driver inquires, looking in his rear-view mirror.

I'm hoping he's getting to the limit of his conversational English. 'I get dressed now.'

'Okay.'

Heading south on the 57D I'm squirming free of my still wet swim trunks, drying the essentials with the sleeve of the terrycloth robe, and squirming back in underwear and chinos. The t-shirt is less of a problem. Sneakers and socks are no problem whatsoever since they are back in the bottom half of the locker. Flip-flops will do.

The taxi hits a steady clip, the driver taps the steering wheel and sings some tune I could never hope to understand. The three hours crawl. I relive the reality warp again and again with no mind to make any concrete conclusions about who did what and why. All I want is to get the hell out of the country.

The taxi fare empties my wallet of its pesos. I leave the robe as a tip.

'It belong to *La Gruta*,' the driver points out.

I shut the cab door behind me. End of conversation.

I arrive at the Air Canada counter with wallet, phone, notebook, and passport. I plank all four on the counter. My minimalist packing raises the agent's eyebrows.

'I'm on the Thursday flight.' I grab another breath and croak a second time, 'I got to get to Canada today.'

Now he's staring at my neck.

'My wife is staying a few more days,' I manage. 'She's got the luggage.'

It doesn't account for the neck. Red, I suspect. Bruised, maybe. I don't give a shit. I just need a ticket.

'Reservation number?' he says, following an extended perusal of the passport.

After a frustratingly sluggish search of my phone I come up with it. The fellow copies the number into his computer.

Fast-paced clicking. Then, 'Ah,' with an edge of verbal swagger. 'The return portion of the ticket has been cancelled.'

'What?' I erupt.

'Yesterday.'

'I didn't cancel it.'

'But you weren't the purchaser,' he announces, as if to confirm any suspicions he has about me. 'That person did.' His eyes return to the screen. 'That would be…that would be Gabriela Ximena Este…'

'The bitch.'

'Mr. Si-nar, I would ask you to refrain…'

'Synard. My name is Synard. Book me a ticket.' I fish my credit card from my wallet and flash it in front of him.

As much as he might want to deny me a ticket, he has no justifiable reason. I stare at him until his eyes return to the screen.

His keyboarding stalls. 'We have just the one flight. Leaving at 1315. You're cutting it rather close.'

'No luggage to check.' As if the bonehead needs reminding. He looks up. 'Let's see if there are any seats, shall we.' You willful slug.

There is a seat. There are several in fact.

'Business class?'

You ass. 'Too roomy. I prefer a tighter space.'

'Aisle or window?'

'I don't care.' I omit the expletive.

'No checked luggage.' He notes for the sake of the computer, pauses, then notes again, 'No carry-on.'

The hit to my credit card takes it a cruel leap towards its limit, but doesn't give him the satisfaction of exceeding it.

I pocket my personal items and lay an open hand on the counter for the boarding pass that finally prints.

'Have a good flight,' he says, cheerlessly. 'Let's hope there are no delays through security.'

I turn to go. I'm about to rush off, but turn back for the two seconds it takes to offer up a few final words. 'You're a bloody charmer. I'll be sure to contact Air Canada's CEO and let him know.'

Security is a breeze. A single tray, thinly laden.

I check the time with my phone and calculate I have just enough to rush through the purchase of one of those ugly neck pillows. Something to cover up whatever. I tear away the packaging, and as I build up speed, anchor it around my neck.

I make the flight, with time to spare. Not a lot, but enough to recover from all that running. There must be an art to running in flip-flops, to cut down on that slapping noise. If I'd had more time, I might have mastered it.

When I've finally settled in my aisle seat, when finally the door is closed, when the plane finally lifts free of the runway, tension drains from me, like the best Lagavulin imaginable had just settled over my taste buds. I am going home, alive.

When it's time finally to order from the bar menu, the Glenlivet is tough to swallow. I slip a hand under the pillow and massage my throat, and it hurts. But by the third Scotch it's somewhat better. I have confidence in a full recovery.

The tanned and more fully dressed fellow seated in the window seat next to me hasn't attempted conversation, thankfully. I suspect largely because the ugly pillow doesn't leave my neck, even with the stream of trips back and forth to the washroom to inspect the colour and bruising beneath it. Or perhaps it's the sight of my bare feet out of the flip-flops as I discreetly exercise them to offset the pain caused, I figure, by all that slapping without arch support.

I need a general restorative—sleep. I am jerked out of it repeatedly, my mind in a snarl trying to come to terms with the treachery at the spa. The neck pillow is no help.

I have zero hope of following the plot line of an in-flight movie. Documentaries and cooking shows are a lost cause. Munching salty pretzels and sipping scotch while pumping classical music through cheap earbuds is the closest I come to setting my mind on an alternate path. Even at that, the five and a half hours it takes to reach Toronto are interminable.

With touchdown comes unbelievable relief. My eyes close and my hands lock themselves against the sides of my head. The pressure is physical affirmation that I've kept my world intact. I remain that way until the shuffling around cuts into the reverie.

The guy in the window seat finally breaks his silence. 'You okay?'

I open my eyes slowly. 'Yeah.' I turn to him and smile. 'O sweet fucking Canada.'

I walk off the plane barefoot, flip-flops in hand. I can do that in Canada and feel safe. I can walk barefoot to my connecting flight, ugly neck pillow around my neck, smiling when people do a double take. Even once at a Mountie.

On a flight now for my home and native Newfoundland. Alert. Confident. Solid as The fucking Rock.

9

IT'S AFTER 1 A.M. when the flight lands. My objective is to escape the terminal without running into anyone who recognizes me. My chances are reasonable.

No lolling about the luggage carousel. A direct getaway through the arrivals area and out the exit where taxis are parked. All good.

I've steeled myself for the cold, but not the icy slush. So much for singing the praises of fall weather. In my absence snow has fallen, followed by rain, which has turned to ice and been sprinkled with salt. The frigid muck seeps over the perimeters of my flip-flops. My freezing feet are in the car with the door closed before the driver has had the chance to exit and make a pointless attempt to assist with luggage.

'Lost,' I explain. Which is technically not a lie. 'They'll deliver it if it ever shows up.' My final few words are mutated by a sudden jolting shiver.

The driver whips his head around and stares at me. 'Mr. Synard.'

Ivo. Ivo Ozols. What the hell? I rid myself of the ugly neck pillow.

Ivo and I have a history. A not-so-pleasant history for

which he almost ended up behind bars.

'I've started driving taxi, Mr. Synard. This time for real.'

'I thought you had fucked off back to Latvia.' To put it succinctly. 'The cops have your number.'

'Me and Ash are saving up. We'll get there.' That would be Ashley, the flighty girlfriend.

He pulls the taxi away from the curb. He knows my address only too well.

It's a messy night weather-wise, but agonizing though it is, the drive takes less than fifteen minutes from the airport. Ivo pumps up the heat and by the time we're parked in front of my house my body temperature has returned to normal. I dig out my wallet.

'I got it, Mr. Synard.' I hold up the money anyway. He refuses to take it. 'The least I can do.'

He's right about that. I open the car door. 'Stay out of trouble, Ivo.'

I step out of the taxi and into more slush. Deeper this time. When I drag my feet through it, it sucks off the flip-flops. 'Sweet fuck.'

Ivo is out of the car in a flash. I forgot just how tall he is. He towers over me, getting a bare head-to-bare feet look at just how unprepared I am for the weather. 'Grab on to me,' he insists.

Anything to get the hell out of the freezing slush. 'I'm good,' I tell him, after lunging onto the sidewalk and hobbling through the snow, up the few steps to the front entrance.

I'm anything but good. My bare feet are blocks of ice planted in the snow. I'm poking around vainly where I had been keeping the key when I realize I'm not wearing the jeans that have the coin pocket and therefore I don't have the bloody key. It's way the fuck back in Mexico.

There's another key, hidden outside the house, in a secret spot near the back door. In case of emergencies, which this is definitely one. Rather than plow barefoot through the snow to retrieve the key, I enlist Ivo.

I bombard him with instructions on where to find it. It involves three coordinates—a wooden post, a triangular-shaped rock, and a half-empty Glenfiddich flask. It's complicated. I wasn't about to hide it someplace obvious.

Now further complicated by the dump of snow. It takes Ivo ten bloody freezing minutes to return with it. But the dogged young bugger comes through.

With me inside the open door, morbidly stiff and desperate to thaw in a hot shower, he's not about to hang around. 'You're a lifesaver, Ivo.' Not words I ever thought would make it past my lips.

'No problem, Mr. Synard.' He shakes my numb hand with his own. He's off, back in the taxi to continue his night shift. He blows the horn and jerks the vehicle through the slush and onto the street.

My tortured body, rid of its trio of flimsy garments, drags itself beneath the tranquilizing hot water lashing the shower stall. I could stay there forever.

When I drag myself awake I have no idea what time it is.

No idea what day of the week it is. I pat a hand about the night table for my phone. Just after 11:00. Wednesday. Yes, it's Wednesday. Yesterday, Tuesday, was the spa day from hell. I drop Nick a quick email and fall back to sleep.

An hour later I'm inspecting the neck in the bathroom mirror. The bruises from the savage stumps of fingers have darkened. But there are not a lot of them. It could have been worse. The low ball kick saved the day. I straighten up in front of the mirror. Then replay the flurry of moves that did the job on the little fucker, with not quite so much energy.

'Dad, you okay? How come you're back early?'

I grab a towel and hang it tight around my neck and make for the stairs. It's lunch break at Nick's school, a ten-minute walk away.

He meets me partway down the stairs. I hit him with a high five.

'Dad, man, what's with the feet. They look like hell.'

An overstatement, but at least he hasn't laid eyes on the neck.

'How did they get so swollen?'

'Really? They don't feel swollen. Red maybe. Too long in the shower.'

He's not buying it. Attention moves away from the feet.

'You sure you're okay? Your face looks off.'

'Off?'

'Puffy. Red. Under your chin it's kinda purple.'

He'll have to live with lies. 'Sunburn, I guess. Mexico was hot. You know me. I was never good with sun block.'

I lumber down the stairs ahead of Nick, who is full witness to the graceless descent.

I have a story and I stick with it. Over time my son has learned that arguing with his father serves no real purpose. Have a difference of opinion, but move on. Focus instead on what matters, not minor details that don't affect what's happening in his own life. I might be a bit "off," but in the long run it doesn't amount to anything. I'll get back to myself in my own good time. So meanwhile let's turn our minds to things that matter.

'Let's make some lunch. You must be starved.'

'Dad, something happened, didn't it?'

'Scrambled eggs. Back bacon?' Nick and I love our back bacon, but we don't have it often, knowing it's not great for us. It's become a forbidden treat.

'Something you're not telling me.'

This is new.

'For some reason.'

A not-so-subtle turn in attitude.

I ignore it. 'I told you. Mexico was hot. This time of year, I wasn't used to it.'

'You're hiding something under that towel.'

What is this? Overnight he's game to take me on? Like his age has leap-frogged all of a sudden.

'Self-conscious. It's blistering a bit. I'd rather deal with it myself. I made a stupid mistake not putting on sun block…'

'Let's see. It's not getting infected, is it?'

Fake buying into it, but push in the other direction. I sit down at the kitchen table. He sits straight across from me.

He stares me down. I look beyond him for answers, in vain. The seconds crawl on.

The towel comes off.

Nick does a double take. 'Fuck, man.' That's new, too. The f-word in front of his father.

'It's not as bad as it looks.'

I work my way into the whole story. Most of it, at least. Culminating with the attempted murder and my getaway. I offer an abbreviated version of the one-two-three tactic that got me free of the little bastard.

When I sit back down Nick leans across the table for a closer look at the neck. I detect a certain pride in his old man for the way I outmanoeuvred my potential killer. That coming from a son who is close to tears.

'You should see a doctor.'

I should, but I won't. A doctor would ask too many questions. 'Bruises are fading. Neck a little stiff, but no permanent damage.' I rotate the neck first one way, then the other to prove my point.

The kid's skeptical. That I can deal with. His willingness to keep it between the two of us is the issue. Blurting out the story to his mother would not be good. The boyfriend getting wind of it from someone other than me would be worse. I make Nick promise not to tell.

"What about Gaffer?' he says, as a joke I assume. Although the dog, in his own way, has been known to let the cat out of the bag.

I'm the one to tell Olsen. He knows I'm back, of course. He knows I'm back early, and for some unknown reason.

I schedule an appointment to see him at his office for later in the afternoon. Fortunately, turtleneck sweaters are back in style.

He insists on seeing the bruises. I hesitate, but in the end oblige. Contusions, he prefers to call them.

Whatever. 'It could have been a lot worse.' A failed attempt at downplaying.

'You could be dead. Not many people around. Likely they had figured a way to get the body off the site without being seen. And dump it. No trace of you ever again. Happens in Mexico all the…'

'What do you mean they? I'm not 100 per cent sure Gabriela had anything to do with it.'

Olsen looks at me with that "Inspector" look he draws on when he needs it. 'You're in denial.'

'Her calling out when it happened was faked?'

'Was it loud enough to be heard by anyone except you?'

'You figure she set it up and Antonio supplied the hit man?'

'Would make more sense. To me.' The latter two words meant to soften the charge of gullibility on my part. 'Why else would she have cancelled your flight?'

Of course I had thought about that. On second thought, the 100 per cent might be the better choice. 'You're saying she lured me to Mexico to have me killed. Still doesn't entirely make sense. To me.' Pause. 'If I had disappeared, suspicion would be directed straight at her.'

'To which she would plead complete innocence. Who else knew you two were going to the spa?'

Nobody.

'The statistic on unsolved disappearances in Mexico is very high.'

To put it mildly. I knew that.

'There's a basic question here we're missing. Why would anyone want you dead?'

'You tell me. I need all the opinions I can get.'

'Someone figures your nose is in the wrong place. You're raising suspicions about who killed Simón, and before you go any further, they put a stop to it. Better it happens in Mexico than Canada, for obvious reasons.'

Olsen starts to make sense. But only to a point.

'Okay. Let's say you're right. Let's say I had suspicions Antonio arranged to have the job done on Simón. You got to remember Gabriela was promoting that herself when she was in Newfoundland. And she only added to it with her phone call. Then the second day I was in Mexico, she took me straight to Antonio.'

'And the next day you disappear. No trace. Dead. Problem solved.'

Is there any need to be so blunt? I'm not used to feeling disposable.

'We're dealing with a specific criminal mindset. Violence serves a distinct purpose, and the chances of paying for it are minimal.'

I spend few seconds with his logic. 'Where do we go from here?'

'Good question.'

Slightly condescending, but I'm in no position to counter-attack. 'I'm thinking we need to work on Gabriela, get her figured out, one way or the other.'

'Your phone made it out of the country, I assume. Have you checked for missed calls?'

I nod, and in front of him I check one more time. The fact that Gabriela hasn't tried to reach me would seem to make the likelihood of her involvement in the attack 110 per cent.

'We'll phone her,' Olsen says. 'Let's see what she's up to.' Which throws me for a loop.

I clear my throat. The two of us. Cohorts of a sort? 'I take it the near-death experience gives me a new status.'

'You're key to the investigation. To be candid about it.' The consummate professional, Olsen.

We compare contact info for Gabriela. We settle on her cell number. Olsen will do the talking. He'll use speaker phone and I'll listen in.

The effort goes nowhere. Not even the option of leaving a message.

'Try her home number.' Which only I can supply.

Three more rings and still not looking good.

Then a very quick '*Sí.*' I recognize the voice. It's Josie.

I mouth *housekeeper*. Dumbfounded. Too many syllables. *Maid, maid.* Olsen nods.

'*Señora Ojeda, por favor.*'

Flawless accent. What is this, Olsen speaks Spanish? Another reason he's useful to the RCMP?

'*La señorita Ojeda,*' Josie corrects him. Obviously he lacks an understanding of the nuances of the language. That and Gabriela's self-image.

Josie can't seem to get any more words out. Then an emotional torrent ensues.

'*La señorita Ojeda está en el hospital. Ella fue atacada. ¡El diablo le rompió la nariz! ¡Un desastre! ¡Su cara nunca será la misma!*'

He holds his palm tight to the phone. 'In the hospital with

a broken nose.'

'*Por favor, dile que lo siento mucho.*' Olsen says, and hangs up without having to tell the distraught housekeeper who called. Likely a good thing.

'Attacked. Apparently.'

Attacked? I'm not sure I buy it. 'The maid's lying.'

'Possible. But I doubt it. If there is a cover-up, the more people in on it, the greater the chance of someone blowing the cover.'

Two investigative minds at work. Feels decent.

'It would explain why she hasn't called.'

'There's a way to find out.'

Interpol. Is he talking Interpol? The big guns for a broken nose? Probably not.

'It would take time. We haven't got time.'

What we got is the pair of us determined to get to the bottom of this shit.

'Say the broken nose is legit. Who attacked her? The guy who attacked me? That means she wasn't in on it.'

'You think if he attacked her, all she'd get out of it was a broken nose? I don't think so.'

Which means she's back to being in on it. 'So what's with the broken nose?'

I feel the shit flying around in a circle.

'Consider this. You escape. She's pissed off because the guy screwed up. She lays into him. Which, we both agree, could be vicious. He defends himself and her nose gets broken in the process.'

Dead air between us. The best scenario so far? We seem to agree. The shit shows signs of settling.

We leave it there. For now. The inspector is a busy man. He needs to report to the RCMP. Plus he's got other cases that need attention.

I don't. I have time to sit, down coffee, and recentre my life. We shake hands as I leave the office. An impressive grip, but my own holds up well. Our relationship has had its barriers. I feel this meeting caused a few of them to break down. I can honestly say, setting aside the ex-wife business, I've come to appreciate Olsen for the sharp cop that he is. Teamwork counts for a lot in his business, and Olsen has the smarts to work through our differences for the sake of the case.

All this calming my mind, I return to the house. Gaffer is alone and in need of a walk. Sunshine and warmer temperatures have returned to the city. We drive to Kent's Pond for our favourite outing. The trail circles the pond and there are wooded sections of it that make a dog and his master think they are completely alone in the natural world. The invigorating smell of evergreens, the late afternoon play of light through the branches, a fall crispness underfoot. A million miles from Mexico and I'm breathing freely again. And walking free of pain.

After I drop Gaffer back home, I set out to walk up Signal Hill. The slush has given way to mostly clear sidewalks, always a treat in the capital city. I feel the need to surround myself with the extraordinary landscape I inhabit. It's time to put the several days just past firmly out of my conscience. Time to let the soul attune itself once again to the rhythms of my homeland. Yes, and time for a little cardio and time to ease back into the regime.

Iconic Signal Hill is a workout, not a ramble for the weak-willed. I maintain a solid pace, bearing in mind the feet have not long recovered. I know better than to push past reasonable limits, yet I feel pumped at what this psyche of mine is capable of. There was a time when a lack of self-confidence played games with it, but that is definitely behind me. Mid-life crisis is passé, no longer there to raise its ugly head.

Which generates the urge to unzip my jacket, roll down the ribbed collar of the turtleneck and let the healing powers of

Mother Nature have at the contusions. Cold but healthy, restorative, damn liberating.

Pay no mind to the curious passersby. Focus on the climb, the 150 metres or more of elevation. Stride up the final incline, troop the walkway past Cabot Tower, momentary home in 1901 to Guglielmo Marconi. (I'm never entirely out of tour guide mode.) Find a vacant spot from which to look out over the drama of the city as the winter equinox steadily approaches, and breathe, breathe in the fact I'm alive and well and able to follow the walkway until I'm in sight of Cape Spear, the naked eastern limit of the vast, teeming continent of North America. Well done!

The walk back is less dramatic. There's the temptation to stop at the Newfoundland Chocolate Company Café and once more revel in a frothy cup of their Jigs n' Reels hot chocolate. But renouncing it puts me a step ahead in the regime game, and that with three hours to go before the fasting buzzer sounds. I'm nothing if not hard-boiled.

Farther down the hill is the Geo Centre, which appears to be closing up shop for the day. And not much further on, the Emera/Grad complex. Here I trim my speed. I'm wondering what Jón might be up to.

Maybe I'll give him a call. Any classes would be over. A bit early for supper. Maybe go for a coffee? Black. There's a place at the bottom of the hill. Why not? It's worth a try. I'm all for acting on impulse.

Inside the main door I scroll through my contacts. His three-letter, accented name makes for a quick find.

Takes a while but he answers. 'Sebastian.'

'Já.'

My sense of humour is gradually returning. It throws him off momentarily.

'I have been expecting you to call. How are you?'

'I've been away. Mexico.'

There is a hefty pause, and when he does speak, a stiffness to his tone that wasn't noticeable before. 'Mexico. What makes you go to Mexico?' And a crack in the fluidity of his English.

'I'm downstairs in the lobby. You got time for a coffee? I'll treat you. How about the Battery Café?'

Another gap, almost as long as before. 'Okay. *Bless.*' Without enthusiasm in either language.

I'm not sure what to expect of him when he emerges from the elevator. What I observe is a young man working hard to look at ease with the idea of the two of us hanging out. No, his stress is not normal student workload stress. It is not from pulling an all-nighter to finish an assignment. Jón is keyed up and triggered to unload on me. I can feel it.

He waits until we're seated in the café. We've claimed a corner by ourselves, two cortados, topped with froth art and freshly delivered to the table. He's never had one before. I've skipped black coffee in favour of something more likely to jumpstart conversation.

'Spanish. Only my second. The first in San Miguel de Allende, two days ago. Enjoy.' An abbreviated start. I want him to take the lead.

'Why did you go to Mexico?' His English has improved. The question has obviously embedded itself in his mind.

'Gabriela. She paid the shot. Well, half of it. She insisted I go.'

He seems to have braced himself for the answer. He takes a sip of the coffee. His grip on the cup is tighter than it needs to be. But no comment forthcoming on the cortado.

'Why did she want you there?'

'The substratal question.' I like the geological connotation. I have been wanting to use that word for some time.

The wordplay exceeds the limits of his English vocab, regrettably, and only confuses him. Enough with the footnoting. I need to get to the root of the matter.

'I know the answer,' I tell him. 'Now I do. If I had known it at the beginning I might not have been attacked and barely escaped with my life.'

'*Fokk!*'

No need to guess at the translation. Jón takes a sudden, audibly thick breath.

On the exhale, another, less intense '*Fokk.*'

I put it to him. 'You're telling me you suspect Gabriela had something to do with Simón's murder?'

He shakes his head. With each uneven breath he's closer to getting past the expletive.

One more prompt. 'What did you tell her about me?'

'I'm sorry. I needed the money.'

'You needed what?'

'Five hundred. That was all. University is expensive. It saved me from going to my father again.'

Fokk is right.

'I didn't have much to tell her. She wanted to know what you were saying, where you were going with the investigation. Just what we talked about on the trip. That was all.'

'You mean you talked to her right after the trip?' I'm stunned.

'She called.'

Stunned and pissed. What the hell? Which confirms she knew my sights were on Antonio. Which confirms she figured he would want to put a stop to it. And, since they were buddied up, she set the lure to get me to Mexico. All calculated on her part. As Olsen said. Cold-blooded and calculated. The sex and all. 'Sweet *fokk.*'

'I'm sorry.' Repeating it doesn't help.

'Why the hell did she hire me in the first place?' I'm thinking aloud.

'I wonder that, too.' As if agreeing with me does anything to redeem him. He's quick to add, 'She's a control freak. She knew what direction you were heading. This way she'd control how far you'd get.'

Brain repositioned. Not as *fokked* up as I thought.

I lay out the episode in the spa. In all its bloody awful detail, culminating in a quick turn down of the turtleneck. He winces. As he damn well should. There's no amends to be made. The bugger needs to feel the brunt of his decision to rat on me.

'Had I known what she was up to…'

I raise a hand in front of him. It's as far as I am willing to let him go. Let it pound in his head for a while. One day I might be willing to set it aside, but not yet. Not until I'm over it myself.

The cortados are finished, as if undeserving of an opinion. We're out the door and off in opposite directions. No handshake, no see-you-later.

All the way back to the house, I'm reliving what just transpired. I don't have a fix on Jón. I thought I did, but there's a crosscurrent of discontent that I still haven't figured out. General student malaise? I think not. Still working through confusion about his sexual bent? Maybe. I need him to level with me. I find my hand unconsciously massaging my neck the nearer I get to home. A complication unresolved. Maybe I won't be seeing the bugger again.

Gaffer comes running when I unlock the door. Plus there's the smell of fried bacon wafting toward me. Nick appears in the hallway, a spatula in hand. Apparently he went to his mother's after school, then made his way here with the dog and a backpack load of clothes.

'No school tomorrow. A PD day for teachers. I talked to

Mom, convinced her it's better for me to be here than home alone all day.'

I can imagine the phone call. On a normal days she wouldn't be giving an inch, but Samantha is a school principal and knowing her and PD days, her mind is overloaded.

'Where you been?' he says, sidestepping past the explanation.

'Needed some exercise. Trying to get the old bod shipshape.' Which is intentionally quaint, to prompt derision from the son and sidestep his own round of probing questions.

In the wake of the derision, he adds, 'Did you see a doctor?'

'Didn't see the point.'

He's not buying it even when I remove a sock and display an unswollen foot. 'Still a bit red,' he says. 'What about the neck?' I put that on display as well.

'What are you cooking?'

Not so easily diverted from the neck. 'I figured you'd chicken out on going to the doctor. But at least do better than an ugly turtleneck.' He digs into his jeans pocket. 'I brought you something.'

He tosses it to me. A present of curious multicolour appearance. I take it out of its cellophane pouch—a piece of stretchy material, some kind of jazzy, patterned microfabric, all wavy blues and orange. Is this a joke?

'Open it up.'

It opens out into a tube. I push my hand through the centre of it so it bunches around my arm. 'Now what?'

'Skateboarders and skiers wear them a lot.'

'That leaves me out in the cold.'

He forces a smile. 'Works around your head. Or your face. And your neck. Get it, neck.'

'Nothing if not versatile.'

'Ditch the turtleneck, Dad. Try to look cool. It might work for you.'

I'll ignore that. I'll ignore the fact that a teenager is dispensing fashion advice to a grown man, who in his day, was the embodiment of cool. Remember when neon was all the rage? I practically lit up Gander.

It would appear I have no choice but to jettison the turtleneck in favour of this neck...apparatus. Nick insists I have a look in the bathroom mirror.

'Wicked,' he delares.

I wouldn't go that far. I angle my neck in various directions. It does the job of coverup. I will go as far as admitting it adds a certain rakish quality.

He laughs. 'Rakish?' He's still laughing. 'Rakish. I like it.'

'Does this indispensible fashion accessory have a name?'

'Depends on how you use it.'

Am I surprised?

'If I were you, I'd call it a neck sleeve.'

I detect condescension. 'And if you were not me?'

He shrugs. 'Makes a cool balaklava.'

We'll leave it at that.

Neck aglow, I turn my attention to the kitchen. Nick has assembled grilled cheese sandwiches, ready for the frypan. He's mixed together a combination of shredded cheddar, Havarti, and Gruyère, and topped it with Brie. (Thanks to his father, he's moved far beyond the insipid processed cheese slice.) We've made them before, but not with this particular combination of cheese. He's also tucked bits of bacon between the bread, then spread the outside with a mix of butter, mayo, Parmesan, and grated onion before frying one side, then doing the same for the other.

I'm liking what I see. I'm liking the fact that Nick has gone to the supermarket and bought extra cheese and put all this effort into making something he knows I'll like. Just to help me through the crap that's gone on over the past couple of days.

We sit at the kitchen table, in front of each of us a sandwich plus a pile of matchstick fries he's baked in the oven with sea salt and garlic. I look across at him and tear up. Like a bloody fool. Hard to hide, unlike the neck. Not that I even try. Nick walks around the table and hugs me hard. 'What you did to that guy was awesome. Back kick to the nuts. That took guts, man.' He's half on the bawl himself. 'Promise me you'll be more careful. Promise you won't get into shit like that again.'

The grilled cheese and fries bring us back to ourselves. They're damned good. I make sure he knows. Gaffer agrees. Gaffer likes his cheeses, and the odd fry.

'You're doin' good?' More for something to say to him than anything.

'Yeah, I'm okay.'

'You and Tyler still friends?'

'He had a fight with the girlfriend. They broke up.'

'It happens. So you see more of him.'

'Kinda.'

Might as well say it. He knows it's what I'm thinking. 'Still think you might be gay?'

Nick's ready for it. 'Who knows. We'll see what happens.'

I start to laugh. In a loving way, which makes him chuckle. I'm thinking, this is good, this is healthy. He's making it work for him. I'm thinking back to when I was growing up. For a young fellow to even hint he might be gay would have been the kiss of death. He'd be the instant target of every shithead in the school.

'So what have you been doing with your free time? When you're not hanging out with Tyler.'

He shrugs. 'I dunno. Not much.' Then he reconsiders. 'Working out.'

We both remember the battle royale I had last year with his mother, over letting him bench press, when he was too young to be doing it. He still is.

'I'm not bench pressing if that's what you're worried about. It's building up my strength, that's all.'

'With weights and stuff.'

'Yeah. I'm being careful. Fred designed a program for me.'

Hackles up instantly. I take a breath and make a lame imitation of a shrug. Unlike last time, I don't freak out.

'It was my idea.'

I can buy that, if I put my mind to it.

I guess if you're living in the same house with Mr. Muscle, it rubs off on you.

'You liking it?'

'Yeah, sure.'

Downplaying it all to hell. Of course he likes it. And of course he's had his mind changed about Olsen.

'Your mother good with it?'

I know I shouldn't be putting him on the spot. Can't help myself. Can't help playing the loser one more time.

'Yeah, she's okay with it.' He looks straight at me. 'She didn't push it, if that's what you're thinking. It just happened, that's all.'

That's right, just happened. And now he's spending more time with the boyfriend than the father, and likely loving it more than playing around in a fucking kitchen.

Not a fraction of what's screwing my mind makes it past my lips. I'll control myself if it kills me. I pick at the fries as if they're all that matter.

'You want me to give it up?'

'No.' Reluctantly. 'I'm good with it.'

'I will. If it's going to make for shit between us.'

Another breath. He is willing to go that far. Willing to give it up just to keep the peace. With that thought I, now, personally and unequivocally, am beginning to feel like shit.

'No, stick with it. Soon you'll be tackling your old dad. And winning. Not!'

Which sounds just like what it is—forced. Neither of us laughing.

Back to the food. Best to move on before it gets even more awkward. Nick eventually turns his attention to Gaffer, who all during this time has been lying low, under the table, no doubt sensing he's better off out of it.

Gaffer takes on a new role, in addition to the many he already performs. Gaffer, the peacemaker. When we move to the couch he stands between us, unwilling to play favourites by choosing a lap. Instead, he launches into a rapid cycle of full-on face licks, one to the other and back again. The Dalai Lama of the dog world. He falls asleep between us, content he has done good, while we haul up Netflix and once again watch *Turner and Hooch*, our favourite dog movie of all time.

Nick goes off upstairs, to bed and to catch up on his social media deficit, Gaffer trailing behind him. I'm left to sit, have a dram of Oban in violation of my dietary regime, and to further question my place in the universe. It's rather like ingesting a triple shot of caffeine.

Okay, so I might have been the shits of a husband at times, but I always thought I made a pretty decent father. When I was growing up, there was a distance between me and my old man that bugged the hell out of me, that I worked damn hard not to replicate. It's a fine line between raising a kid to be straight-up and respectful, while at the same time working to make him the chum you wished you had been with your own father.

And then some guy shows up off the street and parades into the scene that has been exclusively yours and there's fuck all you can do about it. I'm not blaming Olsen. Screwing around with Samantha comes with obligations. Getting along with Nick being number one.

So he works at it. All I'm saying is he doesn't have to work so fucking hard. Leave me room to be the father. Try squeezing me out and there'll be hell to pay. Cop or no fucking cop.

Okay. Decompression time. Gear down a few notches. Pour another dram.

Sleep on it.

I'm awake by 5 a.m., still wired. Inertness is tough to come by these days. The mind has no interest in equilibrium. On the positive side, it's no longer in my head to take a fist to the inspector.

I switch my phone off mute, not that being ringless helped keep me asleep. I notice a text has come in during the night. From Jón. Peculiar, to say the least. Not only is he wanting to reopen communication, apparently the urge to do so came in the middle of the night.

—*We need to talk. TSTB*

Now there's a succinct text. Even at that, the latter part is incomprehensible. I consult *internetslang.com* for a translation. *The Sooner The Better*. Ahhh.

TSTB is one step away from Urgent. Which is good. Still, something is up and I better get back to him a.s.a.p.

—*Okay. Battery Café? Opens at 7:30.*

Ten seconds later:

—*IBT*

That, I figure out. Refusing to double check, despite the fact *internetslang.com* is wide open. I have my pride.

Nick and Gaffer are still sleeping as I get ready to leave the house, and I expect they will remain that way until I get back. I leave a note and lock the door behind me.

In five minutes I'm at the café. Jón is already there, seated, the only customer. A pair of cortados are delivered to the table as I remove my jacket and take the chair across from him. Jón is anxious and set to engage. I barely have time to take a first sip.

No preliminaries. 'I got an email from Simón.'
What's he going on about? I don't need to ask the question. The furrowed brows say enough.
'Last night, about 1 a.m., an email from Simón.'
'Something wrong with your computer?'
'Delayed delivery.'
'I didn't know you could do that.' Actually, I never really thought about it.
'Who gives a shit?'
The man is agitated. Impatiently agitated. 'He sent it the night before he left for Gros Morne. He sent it in case something went wrong.'
He sticks his phone's screen in front of me.
Jón, there's a USB stick taped under the shelf of my locker in the Geo Centre. I want you to be the first to know. Simón
I take another sip of cortado. Jón has yet to touch his. He says nothing. Too painful, to state the obvious.
That leaves me to pick up the conversation. 'He was worried he might not make it back.'
'Alive.' Jón's voice starts to break. 'If Simón was alive,' he says, struggling to regain control, '…he would have cancelled the email after he got back.'
In which case I'll say what needs to be said, as gently as I can. 'He selected you as a confidant. Why you?'
He looks at me like I'm clueless.
Okay, you want to play rough and ready. 'Simón was still crazy for you. Whether you believed it or not.'
It's suddenly turned dicey.
Jón sucks at his coffee. I relocate to the counter and return with a couple of cheese scones. To distract him while I go deeper.
'What happened between you two?'
'Fuck off.'
He also ignores the scone.

But he doesn't just up and leave, like I half expect. I backtrack, do what I can to keep him talking.

'Sorry.'

He looks at me. 'Let's get something straight. I didn't have to tell you about this. I could have just kept it to myself.'

Or taken it to the cops. Which is what he should be doing because if they ever found out that he's told me and not them, he could be charged for withholding evidence.

I don't say that. Because I want be the one to find out what's on that USB stick. If it's anything useful, I want to be the one to hand it over to Olsen and the RCMP. Sometimes blind jealousy has its part to play.

I work at sounding reasonable. 'What's on that stick could lead us to whoever killed Simón. I need your help if we are going to get to the bottom of this. Simón was obviously worried someone had made him a target.'

Emphasis on "we." Jón acts like he's considering it. He's playing a game, one that's not going to take him far. He made the choice of coming to me and for good reason. He owed it to me.

'How do we get your hands on the stick? I take it you have access to his locker?'

'We both did shifts at the Geo Centre, working round our university schedules. He did tours. I did security, after they close for the day, five to midnight.'

'You're still there?'

'I took a break after what happened. I couldn't handle it. They understood. I'm due to start again today. I'm on with another guy, Jason.'

Convenient timing. In any case, I assume he could go in any time and check the locker room. He says he'll wait, until his shift starts.

I can't believe he'd put it off that long, considering how nervous he's still looking.

'I have a mid-term this afternoon. And I have to study for it.'

Nervous and scared shitless of what the stick might reveal.

'If I fuck up on the exam, I'm screwed.'

To be matter-of-fact about it all. There's no convincing him otherwise. I figure he's thinking that what's on the stick is all about Simón and him, too steamy for public consumption, too painful to deal with right away. Definite cause for mid-term fuck-up.

I walk with him back to the grad residence. We're standing outside the front entrance. 'I'll text you,' he says, 'as soon as I get the stick and have a look at what's on it.'

'I'll be in the parking lot. In case we decide it needs to go directly to the cops.'

That's the plan. I give him a stiff pat on the back. Which he doesn't appreciate, but which needed to be done.

Waiting most of the day for the USB-stick drama to unfold still seems to me a colossal waste of time. But he's given me no choice in the matter. He's calling the shots and I'm strung out, on standby.

Distractions are mine to latch on to.

When I get back to the house Nick is still asleep, though Gaffer is downstairs looking frustrated. He's a dog who appreciates routine and is at odds to understand why I wasn't available before now to let him in the backyard to do his business. He stares at me, his words on mute but his expression entirely comprehensible. *What is this? My bladder can only take so much.* I draw back the patio door and he exits, his pride tested but still intact.

Since the regime has already been blown for the day, I see no point in delaying a full-on breakfast. I cut up onions and mushrooms and start sautéing them in olive oil and butter, then await the consequences. Within ten minutes Nick is standing blurry-eyed in the kitchen. He's a kid easily brought to form by the sizzling promise of onions and mushrooms.

He's into making toast before I ask. This was the original regime, even before the breakup with Samantha—unemployed father and his son in the kitchen on a weekend morning, while the mother took the opportunity to sleep in. I was doing all I could to appear useful.

There is no carry over of the tension from last night. Affirmation of my male grudge theory, although when the other male is your son, it gets more complicted. So far so good.

I'm into egg scrambling. Soft and slightly runny, which we prefer, the onions and mushrooms mixed in, together with parmesan and fresh basil, topped on the plate with a sprinkle of Newfoundland Sea Salt. Toast and partridgeberry jam to the side.

If that doesn't draw Nick unreservedly back into the fold, nothing will.

Gaffer hates being left out of the feasting. I take up a dog-size portion. Removing the onion bits is a little tedious, but worth it. Not your nutrition-charged pellets of kibble I know. But nonconformist Gaffer, of course, despises kibble. I'm convinced dogs have a more refined sense of taste than kibble manufacturers give them credit for, and besides, God only knows what kibble is put through to give it a shelf life of a year. We're the ones trained. Trained to think dogs shouldn't eat so-called "human food." Bullcrap I say. Let them enjoy a meal for a change.

Here's my mind—worked up over dog food. I take it as a positive. There is space for something other than all the multitude of possible scenarios that could unfold this evening, depending what's on that stick.

Nick glances across the table, detecting a certain brain cramp. My efforts at normalcy meet reality. I smile and clear my mind of the kibble controversy.

'Me and Tyler are going to a movie later. You can come if you want.'

That's good of him, offering to include his dad where he's likely not wanted. Besides, any loud, frantic, IMAX, superhero blockbuster might just put me over the edge.

'Thanks. I'll take a rain check.'

'Something's up. What is it?'

I've never been good at feigning composure. There is always something that gives me away, like excess enthusiasm about unrelated matters.

'Nothing really. I'm good.'

'You've been traumatized. You need more down time to centre yourself.'

Good God, what's he been doing to come up with this stuff? Whatever it is, it expands his vocabulary.

'Just quoting my counsellor.' He offers a half smile. Though wide enough to include an edge of cockiness.

I had chosen not to bring up the therapy sessions. They've done more than up his self-confidence. Well worth the money. I must tell Samantha.

'You're still not yourself,' he dares to add.

Which leaves me with the question of whether I should tell him about the latest turn of events. I pour myself a coffee, bite into a piece of jammed toast, and decide I might as well. He's owed it.

First I swear him to secrecy, again. He loves it. He's big on intrigue. What I don't tell him is who I have in mind when he takes the oath. Or that it might be a test of our solidarity.

'Okay, so there's this USB stick...' And go on from there. Nick's brain all the time on high alert.

'Wow,' he says, when I finish. 'This could be like the key to the whole shitshow.'

His excitement loosens his tongue. Which it has been doing a lot lately. Words he'd never use in front of his mother. I think he figures it evens out our relationship. Man to man, no longer man to boy.

I let it go. A talk for another time. I'm not about to risk getting on his bad side again.

'I'll come along,' he says. 'I'll wait with you in the parking lot.'

I shake my head and chuckle.

'I'm serious. I'll be your back-up.'

'What are you talking about? I'm there to pick up a USB stick, if it comes to that.'

'In which case, there's no reason for me not to come along. I'll keep you company.'

I don't have much of a counter argument, since I've kept him on top of most everything that's happened so far. I'm thinking it's helping him get over the trauma of the so-called "shitshow." That and whatever the counsellor has been handing him.

'I'll have my phone.'

Which is supposed to somehow bolster his case, like it's a jolt of reassurance for me to know that. I have to smile. Does he ever not have his phone?

'In case you think I'll be bored.'

Right. He's playing all the angles.

Smart little bugger. I smile again, and leave it at that.

After Tyler's mother picks up Nick to drive the two newly rejuvenated friends to the mall, I decide to wing it and see if I can't set myself up for a face-to-face with the prickly geologist Blane. On the chance new info has surfaced within the bleak confines of academia. No point in phoning him; he'll just put me off. My best bet (likely my only one) is to go directly to the univeristy on the prospect he'll be there.

I arrive at his office door to find a message taped just below the aged Peanuts cartoon: *Mid-term results will be distributed at next class. No student office hours until after that. As tempting as it might be to knock at this door right now, you will not be invited in. Cheers.*

I knock anyway. And a second time, in this case with a certain chummy rhythm that might suggest I'm a colleague from down the corridor rather than a student. Professor McKay opens the door.

For a brief second his response is no more affable than if I had been a first-year student with a runny nose. Until he puts on his glasses. 'Sebastian. What the hell. I just called your house. Couldn't get an answer.'

He opens the door wide and motions me in. He positions a chair for me, then installs himself behind his desk.

Not what I was expecting. 'Fire away.'

'Of course you know who I'm talking about when I say Jón Karlsson?'

This could be interesting. 'Friend of Simón. Also a grad student.' I don't want to appear too keen.

'He's a decent student. Not the sharpest of the lot, but not bad. Works hard. Determined.' Blane stops at that. 'This is on the QT by the way.'

QT. Haven't heard that in a few decades. Blane needs to get out more.

'I shouldn't be saying anything. Don't want to influence your opinion of him.'

I'm looking a bit confused.

'Didn't he ask you?' My look doesn't change. 'He used your name as a reference.'

Seriously? Blane must be kidding. Blane, however, is not the kidding type.

'He's applied for a graduate assistantship for next semester. We expect references to be aware they've asked.'

It takes a moment to digest. 'Perhaps they do things differently in Iceland.'

The professor is not convinced. 'I'll deal with that at the interview.'

'I obviously don't have any background in geology.'

'You're strictly a character reference. The other two deal with the academics.'

'I haven't known him for long. Only since the murder.' To add a blunt edge to the proceedings.

The word triggers a slight recoil. Blane is mute for the moment, before coughing up his response. 'I suspect he was hard-pressed.'

As opposed to hard up? Thanks, Blane.

'Foreign students don't tend to meet many people outside the university.'

'He drove with me to Gros Morne. He needed to pick up his car.'

It would seem Blane is aware Simón had borrowed Jón's car. 'In that case, you likely qualify. More than a lot I get. Better than the bartender I had to deal with on the last application.'

I happen to think that some bartenders make excellent judges of character. Of ex-wives in particular.

'Tell you what. I'll give you a couple of days to think about it. I phoned your house just to touch base and set up a time to call back. So let's stick to that. Give me your email, so we can connect one way or the other. I'll have a few standard questions and you add what you want.'

He jots down the address. Which basically brings an end to the meeting from his perspective.

Not so fast. 'Anything new I should know about? Anything new making the rounds in the department in regard to the murder?'

A facial contortion meant to transmit indifference.
'We need to know. Could be a potential lead.'
He's unsure about the "we." But unwilling to ask.
'Some speculation, that's all.'
Speculation can be good. Depending on who it's coming from. I wait him out.
'I don't give much credence to it myself.'
Still waiting.
'One of Simón's professors...whose name will not be told, so don't ask.'
Not even on the QT?
'One of Simon's professors is convinced he was coming on to him. If you know what I mean.'
I'm not a dinosaur, Blane.
'Nothing explicit. Just the one time. And nothing came of it. But maybe it tells you something.'
That he was trying his hand, so to speak. No news there. Anybody who knew Simón knew he didn't play by the rules.
'The professor thinks it was a trial balloon. That, if it worked, it would give him leverage. On his assignment grades. Or his term mark. Who knows?'
'Simón was a top student. That prof from Texas called him brilliant.'
'Maybe so. He wasn't around long enough for us to come to our own conclusions.'
Rather a heartless way of putting it. In any event, they're barking up the wrong tree. In my opinion, and my opinion is backed up with a lot more than what's backing up theirs. I find university types have this overblown sense of their own astuteness.
'That's it? Any more speculation?' At the risk of sounding dismissive.
'That's all I have to say.' A risk that brings an end to the conversation.

Oh, well. There it is. 'Get in touch in a couple of days. I'll do some more thinking about Jón.'

I stand up, at a time of my own choosing. I extend a hand, which Blane is not expecting and which he shakes with less ruggedness than you would expect from a geologist. It's been a very long time since he's seen anything resembling rugged terrain.

I drive home via the Avalon Mall, the city's centre of commercialism, referred to as the "Babylon Mall" by cynics, though rare is the local resident who doesn't darken one of its multiple entrances at least a few times a year. More than fifty years standing and the flash of credit cards there is stronger than ever. When I was a kid it was the uncontested highlight of any visit to the capital city. Remember Woolco? I cut my consumer teeth in Woolco.

I meet up with Nick and Tyler outside the noise fabrication plant called the Rec Room, an oversized, glitzy games arcade of nerve-grinding proportions. Couldn't pay me enough, as they say.

The pair have seen the movie and have had their stint of gaming, leaving them fired and wired. And anxious for me to attend to one of only two remaining senses not yet maxed out. We head for the food court.

Let's just say I'm not a food court enthusiast. But it does have its function, in this case to fill guts and allow the next several hours to be food free. Mr. Souvlaki and Thai Express say all that needs to be said.

All three of us round up our meals. Tyler's gut answers instead to the call of Subway. 'What's up, Tyler,' I ask the Footlong in the face.

It takes him a while to chew all that shaved ham. 'Not much. Ditched the girlfriend.' He pokes Nick with an elbow.

'Or did the girlfriend ditch you?' Tyler expects my taunts.

'You know me, Mr. Synard. I'm a player.' He pokes Nick again.

Either he's entered adolescence well ahead of the game, or he's playing me for all I'm worth. Perhaps both.

'Nick here is my wingman.'

Urban slang beyond his years. I can only imagine what he finds on the Internet to occupy his idle hours.

I've always thought of Tyler as a good kid. A good pal for Nick. Up to now at least.

'I'm only having you on, Mr. Synard.' He hands me a smile. One I can't interpret.

Nick is laughing so much he can't swallow his Beef Pad Thai.

There reaches a point where your understanding of your own kid's world reaches a wall. I'm not there yet, but I see it looming. What will the next few years have on offer, I wonder.

Once I drop Tyler at his house there's a definite lull. I won't say relaxation, because we both are anxious to see how the rest of the day plays out.

Gaffer is at home, holding his bodily functions in check, awaiting the return of his two favourites. He's no doubt in his chair of choice, the one that allows him a view through the street-facing window. When we pull up in front of the house, he's already barking excitedly, something he's likely been doing for a while. Mutts have amazing car sense. My neighbour tells me Gaffer detects the sound of my car's engine long before the car is in sight. Were I ever to make the switch to electric, I'd never be forgiven.

We don't have much time. Enough for Nick to give him a quick walk, while I check my phone for texts that might have come in while I was driving. There's one announcing local liquor stores have Captain Morgan Rum on special. Trash. Another reminding me that tomorrow is garbage collection day, including recycling. Mental note. Another declaring I have yet another follower on my whisky blog. Fanfare.

A text pops up from Jón just as I'm about to close up shop.
—OMW CUS
Back to him: *—FC*
Seamless. I've done a text slang tutorial.
Back to me: *—FC?*
Sweet. Back to him: *—Fingers crossed.*

The walkers show up and it's a quick turnaround to get Gaffer out of his harness and Nick out the door.

'Let's just take him with us,' says Nick. 'He's been alone in the house the whole afternoon.'

Gaffer is all ears. And dead set against his rightful companions deserting him again. I give up before I even start to argue. 'Let's just go.'

Gaffer is bundled in Nick's arms and buckled in the front seat with him, while I've barely had time to activate security and lock the front door. I slip into the driver's seat and Gaffer yelps a short yelp of approval before curling onto Nick's lap in an attempt to make himself invisible.

I've learned not to obsess over the little things. I roll my eyes, exhale loudly, and drive on.

The parking lot at the Geo Centre is clearing out as we arrive. I pull into a slot in sight of the main entrance, but not close enough to draw attention. Within ten minutes of closing time, ours is the only vehicle except for a pickup idling nearer the entrance. But then that, too, is gone.

I assign Nick the purely honourary role of, in the antiquated sense of the word, wingman. He's suddenly stouter, taller, and imbued with a sense of justice. He always was a bit of an actor.

So begins the wait. For how long I have no idea. It all depends, I'm assuming, on the time it takes for Jón to retrieve the USB stick without being noticed by the other security guy. And to then find an opportunity to plug it into his phone—assuming he's brought an adapter—and read what's on it.

A few minutes stretch into increments of ten. Ten, then twenty. By thirty I'm getting antsy. All the time, six eyes peeled for movement at the front entrance, ears pricked for a text. Gaffer has set aside his reserve in favour of status as a watch dog. He's the one with the wherewithal to control the vertical incline of his ears.

It's Gaffer's sixth sense that alerts us something is up. The mutt turns rigid and yelps once, and then again. Nick locks his jaws together with his hand, redeemed about the decision to bring him along.

Sure enough, a few seconds later the door to the Geo Centre opens and Jón appears, surveying the parking lot.

'Hold the fort.' I'm outside in a flash, walking speedily across the parking lot. I don't run, which, by the time I get to Jón, I conclude, made no sense. No other soul around. Just the two of us, now eye to eye.

'You got it?'

'It's inside. You need to see it first.' He's nervous. He's agitated.

'I'll get picked up on the security cameras. What about the other guy? You'll be in shit.'

'No more shit than you'll be in if you don't come inside.' What's that supposed to mean? 'Jason is not around. He's having a nap. We take turns.'

Really? What reason have I got not to believe that?

He urges me on. 'Hurry up. There's no time.' The entrance doors are wide open.

They close behind us. Jón swipes a card and a second set of doors opens. He hurries ahead and I follow. To where? I would have thought to a security office, but not so.

We're in a glass-walled elevator, descending to the Reception Hall, the Centre's grand signature space, the planets of the solar system suspended overhead from a huge black canopied ceiling. Jón takes off, his long strides barely shaving the floor, waving at me to follow him.

This room is straight-out cosmic. All those planets. Always make me feel like a pinprick in the universe.

Jón would have me believe it's all so much dead space on the way to wherever the hell we're going. The bugger won't slow down. And I can't be shouting at him to stop, for fear of waking up Jason.

I spy my favourite spot in the whole Geo Centre and dig in my heels. Not an inch further. Nada. Zilch. Until he talks to me.

Sands of Time. Three transparent columns. One grain of sand equals one year. One with a paltry seventy-five grains—that's us, if we live that long. Another a metre high with sixty-five million grains—to when the dinosaurs packed it in. And the one breathless me is leaning against, shooting to the ceiling, and through the roof if they could have done it. 4.543 billion bloody grains—the earth's birthday bash.

Talk about feeling like a pinprick. 'What the fuck?' I blurt at Jón when he finally realizes I'm no longer behind him.

'You're wasting time. Jason wakes up, we're screwed!'

'Show me your phone. Show me what's on the stick.'

'I forgot to bring an adapter.'

Jesus, I knew it.

'We have to go to where there's a computer.'

'You didn't bring your laptop!'

'I didn't think I'd need it. I forgot.'

'Which is it? Cause neither one am I buying.'

'C'mon, we got to get there.' Now he's freaking. 'C'mon!'

'I'm not going anywhere. Just tell me what was on that stick.'

'You need to see for yourself!' he yells. If Jason didn't hear

that he's too fucking deaf to be working as a security guard.
Jón pulls at my arm. 'Please, Mr. Sebastian. Please!' Like he doesn't know what to call me. Like he's at the end of his rope.
His eyes suddenly swell. From behind me, a pair of hands latch themselves around my throat!
Déjà fucking *vu*! Except this is a monstrous pair of hands.
'Move and I'll break your gawd-damn neck.'
And he's not Mexican. What's with this "gawd-damn."
'Not here,' yells Jón.
What not here? The breaking of the gawd-damn neck?
My head is in a two-handed vice. Do I take a crack at breaking free and pay the price if it doesn't work? Or go along with the bastard and pay the same price, only later.
'No blood remember. You said no blood.'
Jón is fucking well overflowing with cheery comments.
I don't give it another second. 1. Elbow straight into what I thought would be the bastard's gut. His groin instead. Better yet! 2. Foot smashed down on his instep. Except he's wearing thick leather boots that are a match for my Reeboks. 3. Leg bend, kick up and back. Extra high to smash into his balls.
'Gawd-damn!' he coughs up, his hands falling away.
'*Fokk! Fokk!*'
I'm long gone. Bolt. Weave. Swerve. I haven't been this fast since high school hockey. Dash. Lurch. Deke. Sprint.
Sprint right up against a massive wall of rock. And with no dekeing way past it. The whole bloody length of the exhibits gallery. An insurmountable beast of a barrier.
The bloody genius who designed the Geo Centre had its back wall slice straight into bedrock, christening it The Great Wall of Rock. The oversized plaque perched above my head declares "Signal Hill's Rocks Existed 300-Million-Years Before the First Dinosaurs." 550,000,000 fucking years ago.
Either way I'm bloody well not impressed. I swerve around

in one slick motion. To find my pursuers standing three feet away, open hands fixed for the grab.

Jón, the sorry-looking *fokker*.

And the gawd-damn Troy Foster!

Looking nothing like faculty from the University of Texas. Looking nothing like a ground-breaking professor of Earth Science. More of a boorish beast intent on breaking my goddamn neck.

'Balls still aching, Professor Foster?'

'We'll drag him to the loading bay first,' says the oversized prick.

First? I fake to one side, then lunge to the other. Not quite fast enough. This time the corn-fed country boy has his paws latched onto my shoulders. He seethes with revenge, and promptly knees me in the nuts.

The pain is searing. I sink to the floor, unable to clutch anything. He drags me to my feet and drags me on.

I shout and scream. And as loud as my testicles allow, 'Jason!'

'Who the fuck is Jason?' yells Foster.

Jón looks at me and shakes his head.

'You think I hadn't figured that out,' I yell in his face. 'Whataya take me for?'

Foster jumps in, 'An asshole who'd be seeing the light of day if he hadn't poked his fucking nose where it didn't belong.'

'You and Gabriela and Antonio. Didn't manage to fucking off me the first time, so try, try again.' A mouthful, but there's spite curdling the blood.

'Second time, not so lucky. Take it from me, this time you're not playing around with a stump of a Mexican.'

'Antonio would feed your ass to his dogs if he heard that.'

'Antonio had nothing to do with it,' Jón mutters.

'Shut up, you.'

That doesn't go over so well with Jón.

'I won't go through with this.'

'You what! Listen you dumbass, the second you let me through that door you dug yourself a hole you'll never get out of.'

'It was just the two of them. They must have hired that guy in the spa.'

'I said, shut the fuck up.'

'*Fokk*, you're going to kill him anyway. What difference does it make.'

Sobering point, Jón. It puts the next minute in glaring perspective.

My phone buzzes in my back pocket. It's got to be Nick, wondering what the hell's taking me so long.

'Why did you kill Simón?' I bark in Foster's face as his grip tightens and he drags me on, my heels scraping the floor.

'Simón found out they were dealing drugs,' says Jón.

Foster releases one hand and takes a swipe at him. Barely misses. Jón slips beyond his reach. More of his loyalty crumbles.

'Liquid meth. In tequila bottles.'

'You set this up,' Foster barks at him. 'You're in over your fucking head, so shut the fuck up, asshole, and do your job. Or kiss your fucking fellowship goodbye.'

A university spot in Texas. You're kidding me. That was the payoff? No way that's all it was.

I yell his way, 'Keep this up and you'll be doing your PhD behind bars.'

Foster wallops me in the side of my head with the back of his hand.

Jesus! Deadens the dialogue.

Blood gushes from my nose. Sweet. Flood the place.

'You said no blood!' yells Jón.

I know nothing before we've stopped and I'm slumped to the floor. Foster boots me in the ribs. Uuugghhhh! A counterpoint to the agony in my head. There's no hope of me getting up.

'Get me the tape.'

I can barely see the floor two inches in front of me, let alone figure what's with the tape.

Until a strip of it is lashed across my mouth. I had nothing left to say in any case.

And with the subsequent lashing—my ankles, then my wrists behind my back—I won't be walking anywhere or pinching my nose to stop the bleeding. I have faith Mother Nature will clog it up. From what I can feel soaked into the neck sleeve, I've already lost a shitload of the red stuff.

'Gorilla Tape is unbelievable. Almost as good as having my Glock. It won't come unstuck in a million years.'

A million years, Foster. How about a piece of 550-million-year-old rock implanted in the side of your head, Foster. How about Jón buggers off and comes back with a slice of 550 million-year-old rock and drives it through your goddamn skull.

I urge on the Icelander through every ounce of brain power left in me. C'mon, man, you fucked up, now redeem yourself.

I can see his feet—two bricks, unmoving. Jón, c'mon, man, do something!

'I'll tell the police you threatened me,' he says.

'Don't make me fucking laugh. I might be shipped home in a box, but you'll be behind bars so long you'll rot. How's that for a career in geology put on fucking hold?'

Jón doesn't say anything. And it's no bloody advantage to me that shithead Foster hasn't got a jeezly clue that Canada got rid of the death penalty before he was even born.

'When I'm gone you'll clean up the blood off these tiles, you'll do what you can everywhere else, and you'll tell them you had a nosebleed. In fucking fact, I can arrange that right now if you like.'

A standoff.

'So cut the shit and open the goddamn doors so I can dump asshole here in the pickup.'

That would be me. Who can barely move an inch he is so wracked with pain. That kick broke ribs. I bloody well know it every time I breathe. Which, fortunately, is still fairly often. I cough up blood with nowhere to go, an excruciating act in itself. A collapsed lung is a distinct possibility.

Not one worth dwelling on. Shithead wants out of here and that means me keeping him company. What plans he has for my carcass remain a mystery. Not worth trying to solve.

This is where it gets painfully dire. They drag me, broken ribs and all, toward the lip of the loading platform. The pain multiplies tenfold, the Gorilla muzzle sealing me to raving silence, blood and curses frothing at it uselessly.

I hear the initial whirr and rattle of the loading door beginning its ascent. From where I lie, I am about to get the first sliver of the outdoors, before it reaches either of the pricks towering above me.

The rattle has all the makings of a death knell. With me sealed inside my apoplectic self. My mind coiled around what fate is about to serve. I clench my hands into fists, shut my eyes, and plead for deliverance.

'Dad!'

My eyes spring open. Six feet away is Nick's face staring into mine.

'Oh my God, Dad!' Then Gaffer somewhere barking like crazy.

The loading door suddenly stops.

'You fucker,' Foster shouts. Jón lands with a thud on the floor next to me.

'I called Fred!'

I think I hear sirens. Somewhere in my muddled brain there are sirens.

Cop cars screech to a halt outside. Jón forces himself to his feet, drags past my head, and restarts the loading door.

The cops have their handguns drawn, pointed at me, until they get a look at the fix I'm in. That's all they see until the door rises enough to reveal Jón, his hands in the air.

Good cops that they are, they reposition their guns. Two others climb inside the loading bay and draw theirs.

'He ran off,' Jon stutters. 'The guy who did this, he ran off. I locked down the building. He can't get out. He's got no pass card.'

Whether they believe him or not, two cops take off, their guns straight armed in front of them. If I could I would tell them shithead is also armed. With Gorilla Tape.

Jón gives Nick a hand up, Gaffer tight under his arm. Boy and dog are all over me. Heedless of the broken ribs. I am desperate to scream, partly for joy.

Nick is about to rip the tape off my mouth, when one of the cops yells, 'Stop. Wait. Is that Gorilla Tape?'

Jón confirms it.

'You'll rip off his lips. There's an ambulance on the way. It needs a trained paramedic.'

Thank God for the RNC. In the meantime, the cop has a temporary solution. He bends over me, and using a penknife he very carefully slits the tape along the opening of my mouth. Enough that blood oozes out and everyone hears my throaty scream.

Followed by the mumble of two words. 'Broken ribs.' Repeated, for emphasis.

Nick is frantic to help. Gaffer is licking my face all over.

'We circled the building trying to find you. Gaffer wouldn't budge past this spot.'

Jón is terrified. As he should be. Another cop runs off to help track down the jerk of a Texan who was set to do me in.

I don't have enough energy to swear, or to want to swear. I just want the bright smile of a paramedic.

He tells me his name is Dougie. And he knows the proper procedure for removing Gorilla Tape from human skin. I believe him. The first of several causes for relief.

My wrists and ankles are cut apart. I'm ever so slowly eased onto a stretcher. It still hurts like hell. I can hear Nick in the background tearfully answering questions from the cop about how he came to be here.

'You're going be fine, Sebastian. Broken ribs are not much to worry about.'

I look up to find Frederick Olsen on one knee peering over me, together with Ailsa Bowmore looking down from above. Olsen rests a hand on my shoulder and offers a chummy smile.

I can barely draw my lips apart. 'Feel my pain.'

Apparently it doesn't come out that way. Olsen nods his head, his smile even more chummy. 'Fucking pain is right,' he says, quietly, reassuringly.

No point in trying it a second time. I would smile if I could.

Nick returns, standing next to him, while Gaffer has another go at my face.

'Give your dad a few days and he'll be as good as new.' Took the words right out of my mouth. The kid's tears have stopped.

Attention turns swiftly away from me. Onto the returning cops and the outmanoeuvred, beleaguered Foster. His hands in cuffs. Next to the RNC strongmen gripping his arms, the bastard's not looking so pumped anymore. How I wish his return came with a show of bright red corn-fed blood.

The stretcher begins its descent over the lip of the loading bay. I catch a glimpse of Jón, standing, looking at me, wondering what I make of him no doubt, wishing he could fade into the crowd. No chance of that. The cops will have their questions and the grad student better cough up credible fucking answers.

I'm lying in the ambulance, and the world outside is lost to me. We leave the Geo Centre behind, Dougie and I, and head for the hospital.

He's comfort to a silent man. The ride is quick and thankfully smooth. My only wish is for the driver to use the siren, if only once, to make it all real.

My wish is granted. Just a few seconds, but enough to blare my defiance in the face of the unholy mess I've just endured. It's all the world like a thunderous f-word. I smile, if only to myself.

10

YES, I HAD a pneumothorax. Now that I know the medical lingo, it doesn't sound so bad. My left lung collapsed, but it has undergone re-inflation. And, I am pleased to say, without complications. I'm breathing normally again.

A CT scan confirmed three Troy Foster-broken ribs. But no soft tissue damage, another plus. In the negative column: recovery time will be several weeks, with restricted mobility.

There was a time when broken ribs were treated with casts, splints, and tight bandage. That's all out the window. The do-nothing-but-rest strategy offers more pain, but less chance of pneumonia. Hence the need for so-called pain management.

Not to brag, but my pain threshold is high. I'm going nowhere near an opioid, even though the doctor puts it on offer. I'll stick with ibuprofen and ice packs, thank you very much.

'Ibuprofen and alcohol in excess is not a good combination.'

Who said anything about excess? 'And does that include highly refined Scotch?'

The good doctor only smiles before adding, 'Your couch is your best friend, Mr. Synard. Eventually you can start taking short walks. Follow that with light activity. Hold off on lifting anything over ten pounds, and off course, sexual activity is not in the works.'

Of course. I'll make a note. Due to broken ribs, heavy breathing followed by climaxing is definitely out.

However, deep breathing is definitely in. This is the word from the latest healthcare professional to drop by for a chat. Her name is Jasmine. Originally from the Philippines, she has been in Newfoundland for five years and loves it despite the winters. She always gets her winter tires studded and she has a special Filipino way of cooking cod that uses lots of cilantro. Her husband's name is John Paul (after the pope) and they have two children, whose names I would have surely been told had I not steered the conversation to other things, namely, the reason for her visit.

Jasmine is a respiratory therapist. Her ultimate purpose in standing beside my hospital bed is to help me with my breathing. She relays to me that one of the major concerns following what she terms "lung trauma" is pneumonia. I knew as much.

'We need to get you on a regime of breathing exercises.'

'Regimes are one of my strong points.'

'Excellent. Or as my boy, John Mark, would say, *excellento*.'

Nice sideways entry for a proud mother.

'Let's do a practice run, shall we?'

'No problem.'

'Or as my other boy, John Michael, would say, *no problemo*.'

Well done. 'Your family has a lovely way with names, Jasmine. "John" has such range.'

She's pleased. 'We start with a few seconds of deep breathing. Air in through the nose, lungs nice and full, belly rising. Shall we begin?'

In goes the air, lungs over-inflating, rib cage expanding, pain ratcheting up. Grimace. Quick deflate.

'Once again.'

No big deal. The grimace is quite well controlled.

'Relax, breathe normally. Feel the pain subside.'

'*Fantastico.*'

Jasmine smiles again. 'Now we do what we calls huffs. Short breaths interspersed with some light coughs. Ready? Here we go.'

Huff, huff. Light cough. Small grimace. Relax. Huff, huff, light cough. Small grimace. Relax.

'Well done!'

I've exceeded expectations. Always a rewarding hospital experience. Jasmine unzips her carrying case and hands me a print-out of the breathing instructions to take home with me. I pledge to do the exercises every few hours. I've been a good beginning to her day, I'm sure.

'You've scored very well on mental attitude as well. Nice and sharp. I find patients with an extended convalescence sometimes let it get them down. Your "*fantastico*" comeback was excellent. A very good indicator. And you were very quick on the name pattern recognition. Excellent again. It's a little exercise I've developed over the years. Good healing requires the physical and the mental working in tandem. And you are off to a terrific start.'

I nod lamely in agreement. Jasmine shakes my hand, and with her carrying case rezipped, she turns to go.

'*Fantastico.*' It's sounding half-hearted, so I repeat it.

'I'll tell my daughter. She'll love it.' A short wave and Jasmine is gone.

I fit in another grimacing round of breathing before Nick and his mother arrive. The look Samantha gives me I remember from the last time she found me in a hospital bed, which would be not much more than a year ago. A look of concern mixed with disbelief that I could have gotten into such a mess, again. The last time it was surgery for a crushed hip. This time only broken ribs. No comparison.

Nick is more sparing. 'Dad, you're looking good. Way better than you did last night. And your throat bruises have reappeared but they're not bad.'

'Throat? What happened to your throat?'

The blood-soaked neck sleeve is long gone, garbaged in Emergency. 'Nothing much,' I tell her. 'I ran into something.' True. Two perverted pairs of hands.

Samantha has a long memory of my circumventing fact. She sees no point in pursuing the throat bit. The broken ribs are enough of a focus.

'I'm being released tomorrow.' That much is true. 'A little pain, but I'll be up and at 'em in no time.'

'I can help out,' Nick says eagerly. 'Like cook and stuff.'

'That's okay, pal. We'll keep to your schedule. I can order in if I need to.'

Samantha thinks that's wise. She is given to routine. 'We'll keep a check on you.' In other words, you made your bed, you need to lie in it.

'We'll look after Gaffer for a few more days,' Nick says.

Samantha has little choice in that one if she's not to disappoint Nick a second time.

With all that good stuff out of the way, we're flying high. Smiles and generosity all around. Samantha spares the question of why Nick was in the middle of a ruckus with armed policemen. I suspect it made for interesting pillow talk with Olsen last night. She must realize that except for Nick's quick thinking, I might not be here at this very moment, having this vibrant conversation.

She wants to be the one to drive me home when the hospital discharge comes through. Which only goes to show that all is not lost between us. It's a pleasant note on which to end the visit.

Yes, as she confirmed, I do need my rest. Although not

before another self-sacrificing round of breathing exercises.

Home is where the Macallan is.
 The new Scotch on tap. The one I've been saving for an extra special occasion. (Remaining alive qualifies abundantly.) The one that will accompany the next posting for my whisky blog. And, as an added bonus, help ease the frustration of lying about the couch, resting.
 I've settled in with a deep moan and a short, but thoughtful sip of a tall dram. I take my whisky neat, although I've quickly come to appreciate the clink of ice in the ice pack now affixed to my chest.
 These are the joys of recovering from wounds inflicted by attempted-murderer Troy Foster. That's a.k.a. murderer Troy Foster, once the RCMP finishes probing him about Simón's demise. Now that my own life-and-death situation has turned in my favour, I'm desperate to get up to speed on exactly what happened following the showdown at the Geo Centre. Olsen and I exchanged a few emails while I was in hospital. I told him what went down before he got to the Geo Centre, but he's been holding out about what came after.
 Once the ambulance left, Nick and Gaffer were sent home to Samantha's in a cop car. That's pretty much it—the sum total of what he's told me. I figure, now that I'm off the endangered species list, he will get around to more. But just how far will the level of the dram have to sink before that happens?
 As it turns out, not even half way.
 —*Coming by in 15 minutes. Good for you?* That would be a *yes*.
 It is well into the evening of a long day. During the few off-duty times Olsen and I have spent in each other's company, I've managed to steer him from a preference for mild, uninspired Scotch to something more complex. He is a good candidate for conversion.

He arrives on time. But not alone. With him is RCMP Inspector Bowmore. I am doubly blessed.

I'm thinking early forties. Sharp, efficient, and attractive. In that order. And with a considerable amount of cop experience, which, to be candid, tends to be a key factor in any vibes she radiates.

The inspectors take up my offer of the couch, sitting discreetly at either end.

'Normally I like things a bit smokier.' I'm not telling Olsen anything he doesn't already know. I make a painful descent into the armchair opposite them. 'But the Macallan is a classic. Never "Macallan," always "the Macallan." I love it.' I indicate the dram I've poured in anticipation of his arrival. 'And for you, Inspector Bowmore?'

'Indeed. I'll have a wee one.'

I nod to Olsen, who takes the hint, retrieves a glass from the cabinet, and pours her a "wee" one. I have the distinct feeling she enjoys Scotch, and has been so inclined for some time.

Olsen downs a sip and nods his appreciation, before resting the glass on an end table. His seriousness hasn't eased any.

'A second close call, Sebastian.'

'Lucky for me Nick came along.'

'Not good to put the boy in that situation. It could have turned out a lot worse.'

I don't need to be told that. Especially by Olsen.

'It's likely he did save his father's life, if that's any consolation.'

'I'll level with you, Sebastian. You were playing with fire, again, and it was only luck that you weren't chopped into bite-size pieces and dumped into a pit somewhere. What do you think we found in the pickup—a brand new axe and shovel, just waiting to be put to good use.'

'Really?' Even after a prolonged sip, a sobering thought.

'This guy is a nasty bastard.'

He sounds even nastier with that assessment from Bowmore.

'He'd have done whatever it took,' she adds. 'In Texas trafficking in meth is a felony, and with the load he was pushing, we're talking twenty years to life. There is a good chance your Professor Foster will never see daylight outside bars again.'

'So much for a stellar academic career.'

Of the two, only Bowmore smiles.

'And as for his partner, Gabriela, who knows at this point? It's something for the Texas police to take charge of.'

And as for Foster, what now? 'The professor cools his heels here while you wait on them to make their move?' I look to both ends of the couch for an answer.

The inspector takes her rightful lead. 'It's complicated. We got the goods on Foster for last night. Linking him to Simón's murder needs more work.'

More work, I suspect, like searching out a violent past. 'So why do you figure he took a knife to Simón's throat. Just to cover up the strangulation?'

'Maybe that was part of it,' says Olsen. 'In a simple case of strangulation, forensics can tell a great deal about the size and strength of the killer's hands. My guess is there was more to the slashed throat than that.' He won't go any further.

I push it. 'You think Simón wouldn't give him what he was after? Sex?'

'Foster gave Simón access to his research. We know that. Simón used it in the paper he published. We had a Professor McKay at the university analyse it.'

Blane. Hmm, good man. Sorry to have undervalued him. Churchill would have approved.

Bowmore adds, 'Foster allowed it, and likely not just out of the goodness of his heart.'

'In other words he expected something in return.'

'At this point, a theory,' says Olsen.

Isn't it always the way.

Which bring us to the question of Jón. And with it the question of me and Jón.

Olsen puts it to me. 'How did he lure you into the Geo Centre?'

He's baiting me. The cops have grilled Jón. In which case Olsen already knows the answer to his question.

I shrug. *You tell me.*

'The USB stick? The one in which Simón spilled the beans on Foster and Gabriela and nailed them to the wall?'

'I never saw what was on that stick. I turned up, but he never showed it to me. I only found out about the drug business when he blurted it out while Foster was dragging me to the loading bay.'

Olsen looks at me intently, but says nothing.

'You don't believe me?'

'I believe you.' The look doesn't let up. 'You knew about the stick, but you didn't tell us?'

I like to think he's only doing his job.

'Maybe there was nothing on it. The plan was for me to show up at the Geo Centre, and if there was anything, he'd hand it over to me and I'd go straight to you guys.'

'Instead you almost got yourself killed,' says Olsen.

'That wasn't the plan.'

Time to take a break and let the whisky do us all some good.

'So the question becomes, did Jón let Foster inside knowing he was going to kill me?'

Turns out there's a bit more to it than that, according to Inspector Bowmore.

She leans forward. She's obviously relishing the twists and turns of criminal investigation, tackling all the angles. It looks good on her. 'Jón says Foster showed up and threated to kill him if he didn't set a trap for you. So they came up with this story about the USB stick.'

My incredulity is audible. 'You mean there never was a stick?'

'That's the story.'

'Then how did he know about the drug business?'

'He says Simón told him before he left for the Tablelands. Swore him to secrecy. Said if Foster ever found out anything could happen.'

'So why tell him at all? Why potentially make Jón a target.'

'In case something happened to him. He wanted the person he was closest to, to have a clue who did it. Why else? Though, according to Jón, that was never said.'

'So Simón gets killed. And Jón figures he knows who might have done it, but he clams up.'

'He's scared shitless,' says Olsen. 'Foster shows up at the symposium and Jón's practically freaking out. Foster notices how stressed he is around him. Finds out Simón and Jón were more than just pals. He tries having a conversation alone with Jón, but Jón avoids him like the plague, which only confirms his suspicions. Somehow Foster gets his email address. Emails him with an offer to ease his way into a PhD program in Texas. Which Jón interprets as code for "you keep your mouth shut and I'll boost your career, say anything and you're next on the chopping block."'

All that requires a bit of time and whisky to take in.

'Plus he's willing to stand by and watch Foster do the job on me?'

Bowmore takes over. The two together are a class act. 'Not according to him. Jón says he'd planned to let the scenario play out, then when they got you aboard the pickup he'd turn on Foster and, in his words, "smash in the brains of the *fokking* bastard." He would have done the job on him to save you. Got his revenge and never get charged.'

'Are you kidding me? Foster is twice his size and built like a brick shithouse.'

'He had his weapon. Earlier in the day he had planted a rock outside the loading bay. I checked it myself. There was a rock there all right and it could have done the job if Jón got his chance.'

'A big if. More likely Foster would have outplayed him, wrung his neck, and dumped him on top of me.'

'Which is exactly what Foster had in mind regardless,' says Bowmore. There's no lack of confidence on her part.

'I guess you're right.' I guess I hadn't thought of it.

'He wasn't about to leave any witnesses. If he was going to get rid of one body, why not make it two?'

Something else to make room for in a tired brain.

Olsen checks the time. They're also looking exhausted. 'Back at it in the morning,' he says. They polish off the remnants of their respective drams and stand up.

I have one last question. 'What about Jón? He must be on the hook for something.'

'He volunteered for electronic monitoring,' says Bowmore. 'Until we decide what to do with him, whether to charge him or not, he won't be going anywhere.'

'Definitely not Texas.'

Bowmore is amused, Olsen is not.

You got to appreciate a first-rate inspector with a sense of humour. Who just happens to be female.

'Thanks for the Scotch,' she says. The unsmiling, but otherwise obliging, Olsen concurs.

'Anytime.'

'Of course the Bowmore 18 is a favourite,' she adds. 'Have you tried it?'

'Can't say I have.'

She's gone then, catching up with Olsen. I close the door. Could it be that she and the whisky are somehow related? It wasn't only the "wee," but did I not detect a slight Scottish burr in the way she pronounced "bastard"?

I'm back on the couch. Not that sleep is about to happen anytime soon.

There's a book on the end table waiting for me, the one I've chosen for the next posting on my whisky blog. I pick it up and study the cover. *For Whom the Bell Tolls*.

A pairing with the Macallan Classic Cut. No surprise for the few people who read my blog—Hemingway again. Whisky, like books, come and go, but a few remain classics. A novel of bloodshed, but a novel of love.

It fills my urge to acknowledge, with great relief, and an exceptional dram, that the bell hasn't yet tolled for me.

The morning is the time to set two regimes aggressively in motion. If I'm going to get over this, I'm going to come through in top shape. Half-hourly rounds of deep breathing offset the urge to eat.

Hunger in turn offset by painless interaction with my laptop. I have been neglecting my other life, that of tour guide, and there is planning to be done in anticipation of the new year when I roll out my line up of tour offerings for *On the Rock(s)*.

I've been toying with the idea of extending the tours beyond St. John's. Well beyond, as a matter of fact. The Bonavista Peninsula has come to mind and stayed there. Plenty happening in that neck of the woods and barrens to entice a crowd of mainlanders eager for Newfoundland culture—theatre, food, art, and music, all roundly complemented with the usual stunning scenery and extraordinarily friendly inhabitants. Theatre festival in Trinity, craft brewery in Port Rexton, puffin colony in Elliston, moose burgers at the Bonavista Social Club—

the list of possibilities to fill a three-day tour grows and grows. The planning takes hold.

Only interrupted by a string of text messages. One a weather statement alert. (Practically a daily occurrence in Newfoundland.) Followed by notification that local liquor stores have Old Sam's Rum on special. (Newfoundlanders revel in their rum. One brand or other is forever on special.)

The third text, from Jón. (Bit of a jolt.)

—*Possible to get together?*

Good question. Possible, but whether it's wise is another matter. One I'll have to think about.

So, here's Jón, potentially the reason for two near misses on my life, wanting to rendezvous with the intended prey.

He, for what it's worth, has another story. Likely to save his own hide??

Definitely more than one question needing answers.

In the end, what's there to lose by hearing him out? The PI in me has not disappeared just because I have mobility issues.

—*Come by my house after lunch.*

I add an address. Jón showing up here will generate a report to the cops. Something to enliven the whisky talk next time around.

The doorbell rings. Definitely not a toll.

Jón is shrouded in apprehension. Understandable.

He looks especially foreign, so far out of his comfort zone that I'm not sure he will be speaking English when he finally opens his mouth.

I point him to an armchair. I have no intention, however, of wasting whisky on him.

'*Fokk* it, Mr. Synard…Sebastian. I'm sorry.'

Forgiveness in any form is not in the works. 'What exactly are you sorry for?'

'For helping get you in this shit.'
"Helping" as a qualifier is not in the works either. The same goes for "shit."
'This quote, unquote "shit" almost got me killed. Twice.'
'The first time I had no idea that would happen. The second time I had a plan.'

It's obvious he's gone over this a thousand times.

'I heard about your plan. The cops told me.'

'You might not believe me, but it's true.' The pitch rises. 'I was prepared to kill that bastard!'

There's a viciousness in the words, unexpected rage, given what I know of him.

Could be fake fury. He needs to save his own skin, and having me convert to his side would definitely help the cause.

'Listen, Jón, you know where I'm coming from. Feeling damn lucky I came out of it all with a sore neck and three fuckin broken ribs. You appreciate that I'm sure. Because if you don't, you might as well stand up right now and walk through that door.'

He stares at me, wordless for the moment. He stands up, walks toward me, and puts out his hand.

The wait is noticeable, but in the end I succumb.

'We have a saying in Iceland. *Hataðu hegðunina en ekki manneskjuna*. Hate the behaviour, not the person.'

A long pause. 'Nice.' A very skeptical "nice."

Are his words anything more than a pre-planned, contrived interjection? The jury is out.

Jón turns toward the door. He doesn't reach it before a dog comes bounding in and starts jumping at his leg, zealous for attention.

Nick follows. 'Sorry. Thought it would only be Dad.' He takes Gaffer in his arms and retreats a bit.

'Remember Jón?'

Nick's not sure what to say. He sits with Gaffer on the couch near me. The dog settles between us.

Jón's eyes turn to Nick, appreciating, it seems, what it is to be a kid.

Nick looks back at him, but doesn't respond.

'Whatever you do, whatever you want for yourself, be good to your dad.'

That's it. Jón turns and walks out the door.

Nick and I look at each other for a few seconds.

It's Gaffer who brings us out of the uncertainty. He has his best buddies on either side and neither one of them is interested in him. He runs the guilt trip, and of course, wins. With a scratchfest behind his ears and along his belly.

'So,' says Nick, 'what will we cook?'

'Your call.'

He thinks it over, until a slow smile unfolds. 'Tex-Mex.'

I tighten my lips to keep the language under control. 'You…'

He tightens his fists and fakes a few punches. 'C'mon, man, broken ribs and all.'

'You little dickhead.'

'Size discrimination.'

All I want to do is hug my son for all he's worth. His fists turn to open hands. We manage it, reaching over Gaffer, for seconds past the ding of Nick's phone.

Tyler is in need of his attention. My own turns to my email.

Tour business, which is good to see. And a note from Blane. A reminder.

I need that reference by tomorrow, if you can manage it.

That reference for Jón. If I can manage it.

That's the question, the one I struggle with the rest of the day.

Alone in the evening, a touch of the Classic Cut to aid the final thrust to a decision, with only a few minutes before the regime's cut-off time, I type into the screen.

To Whom It May Concern:

And wait and wait, wanting to get it right.

ALSO IN THIS SERIES

One for the Rock